ed by Willow Press
contact: margaretf@hotmail.co.nz

talogue record for this book is available from the National Library
New Zealand.

BN 978-0-473-72685-0 (Hardback)
BN 978-0-473-72686-7 (EPUB)

My Past Be

Margaret

Willow Press

Publish
Autho

This i
are th
any r
enti

A ca
of N

IS
IS

Thank you, John, Beth and Toby, for inspiring me to finish my story, while suffering a personal sadness of my own.

Today is good, but not as good as yesterday

—T E

Part One
Beth

The Blitz

The Second World War had arrived. The 'Blitz' year of 1940–41 in the East End of London, which was being heavily bombed by the German Luftwaffe bombers, was causing widespread devastation. As people emerged from the Underground station, which was being used as a bomb shelter, the skyline was just a haze, as fires were burning out of control. Among the chaos and ruins after the last bombing spate lay the casualties, many women and children, the unlucky ones that hadn't made it to the shelter in time. The dust and ruins were an all too familiar sight these days. It was only when the sirens stopped that people made their way to ground height, to find the horror of the war unfolding. No landmarks were left standing, homes were reduced to rubble, that was if people could fathom where they used to live. Now their lives were likened to a jigsaw puzzle, with thousands of pieces, but where did they begin to fit their lives into a complete picture? Hopelessness overcame all; they were fragile creatures with nowhere to go.

The East End of London was the docklands area, so this was a major target for the Germans. The docks were the hub for imports and war supplies as well as being the most densely populated, so there was the potential for major casualties during the bombing raids. The Germans planned to weaken Britian's resistance and force them to surrender by 'Blitzing' this crucial area. The heaviest attacks occurred during 1940–41, when more than a million houses were destroyed or damaged and many people lost their lives, contributing to the toll of 40,000 British civilians killed by bombing during the war.

My life began in 1936. I was the first child born to my parents, but they had taken in a young lad who was fourteen years of age and who needed to be looked after. He was no relation, a complete stranger, but this is what happened during the war as many children had lost their parents or were separated from them, so others were willing to help. At that time my parents only had me, so John became their responsibility, as he had lost all memory of his past. He could only remember his name being called, then nothing.

Father was exempt from enlisting in the armed services as he worked for the government, so when our house was bombed, he was given a council flat, which became my home. I have only fragmentary memories of the war, but the one thing that did stick with me was the lack of food. Food was rationed, eggs were almost non-existent, and if my memory serves me right, I think we only received one a week. Bread pudding (quite unlike today's bread and butter pudding) was our staple diet, as butter was also rationed.

The landscape was not a pretty one, as complete streets had become graveyards of bombed-out buildings. The odd dog and cat emerged, scavenging for food. But like us humans there was not enough to go around. How our lives had changed; many parents and children were living in public buildings, such as libraries, schools, churches and cinemas – anything that had a roof over it.

My friends' parents stayed living in the Underground as it provided some protection from the bombs. But this was being discouraged by the government as there was the added danger of flooding, gas leaks, disease and panic. In the end the government was forced to supply basic amenities such as toilets, beds and food. My best friend was Alice, and she lived down there with her mother and three brothers. Their father was away fighting the war, and they had nowhere to go, so were forced to live in the Underground. This is where I spent a lot of my time along with hundreds of other families, mainly women and children as the men were defending our country. My dad always felt he was not doing his bit, but his services were needed by the government.

Children were sent away to the countryside; some even went overseas as London was not a safe place for them. No one knew how long the war was going to last or how much more devastation would be caused. My mother was a good person in many ways, competent at such things as cooking and washing, but she lacked the ability to properly care for me. Her maternal instincts never materialised. This was where John played a big part in my life. He saw I was kept clean and fed at the right times. When my brother was born, his workload doubled. Mother just squandered her time; she could never get herself organised. I never really knew what my father actually did for a job, only that he worked for the government.

One day a man knocked on our door and announced he was John's father. They had been separated during the Blitz and it had just come to light that his son had survived and was still alive. He had gone around all the hospital army tents and there was a 'John' listed without a surname, but it was in the same area they had lived, so he held on to hope this was his son. This was the last we saw of John, or even heard from him, so he was lost to us forever we thought. We all wept, especially Mother as now the workload was going to fall back on her. But no, that did not happen. I became my brother's caregiver, making sure he was fed and his dirty nappies changed. Now I knew what jobs John had had to do for me as a young child. I thought of him often, as he was the first person outside our family, apart from Alice, who left a lasting impression on me. Mother talked about John all the time, and although he was no longer with us, he was certainly not forgotten.

My friend Alice and I roamed the Underground every day looking for food that may have been left behind by families who had moved into a council house. My family were considered one of the lucky ones, because with my father working for the government, we were one of the first to get a council flat – unlike Alice's family who like thousands of others were left to fend for themselves. The government couldn't supply housing for those in desperate need, as there were other immediate concerns to be addressed. Alice's mother worked in the munitions factory putting together components for bullets and bombs. Many girls and women, along with men who didn't qualify to sign up as soldiers, were required to work in these factories to keep up the supplies for the war.

As the war was nearing an end the rebuilding of infrastructure was the main source of employment. It was all the talk that the end was in sight as the bombing had stopped so now the reconstruction of homes was the priority. People living in the Underground urgently needed to be housed where the children could feel normal again. Council flats were the quickest way to get housing under way as no one had money to build their own homes. There was no choice, but a home was a home, and it was above the ground. Immediately after the war there was a shortage of construction materials and labour, which slowed down the rebuilding process.

Alice and I had our first schooling in the church at the end of the street as it was mostly still intact, one of the only buildings inhabitable. We were there until a new school was built three blocks away. It was a lot further to walk, but this suited Mother, as I left earlier and got home later so she could fritter a whole day away in her own faraway world.

As the city began to look somewhat normal again, children from host families were gradually returning to the neighbourhood. Alice's three brothers had returned home, so her mother had to give up night work for working the school hours. My mother was not happy when my brother came back, as her life was not about her any more. Father was a great help and bypassed Mother, making decisions that irked her.

Here we were once again; I became my brother's keeper. Father told me I had to care for my brother and make sure he had a lunch made each day. Meanwhile, Mother swanned around doing very little, somehow managing to fill in her day, but come teatime she was exhausted. Although I was called upon a lot to do household duties, I always managed to get my schoolwork done. My father was very proud of me. I didn't know what my mother felt as she never showed any interest in my schoolwork.

It was only now I learned what my father's job was. He worked in a laboratory making the glass vials for vaccines. As sanitation was still being dealt with, infections and medical disorders were pretty well everywhere, so overtime was being worked in Father's laboratory. As the health system deteriorated, we saw less of him, because as a government employee his work came first. Thus, my workload was extended. Several times I nearly came to blows with Mother, but still got no response or help from her; she was a lost cause.

Sadly, Alice's father never came home from the war. Her mother was given a war pension by the government to help feed the family. They were now living in government temporary housing, until further apartment buildings were constructed. Also, charitable organisations were formed to help families who had lost their breadwinner.

One day when Father had a day off, I asked if I could meet up with Alice and visit Victoria Park in the East End with its lovely pond. He agreed I needed a break, so off I went. Alice had some money, but I had none, so she shared with me. We bought an ice-cream and shared a bottle of fizz. We walked to the pond and sat nearby dreaming of how life could be different. It was then she told me she had met a nice boy, and she was sneaking out at night to meet him. She was fifteen and I was fourteen.

"What do you talk about?" I asked her. Alice smiled and told me not to tell anyone, but they were having sex. I was shocked as I knew that adults did that, but children! When I asked what they did, Alice giggled as she tried to explain. I listened but didn't understand half of what she was saying.

"How did you know what to do?"

"My boyfriend is nineteen, so he taught me as he has done it before lots of times. It is fun, Beth."

I still hadn't taken it all in; sex was not something I had even thought about, as I was too busy at home, playing mother. Perhaps I could ask my mother one day to explain, then I might understand it better. I didn't want to seem dumb in front of Alice. We had a fun afternoon, and it was good to be together, as now that she had a boyfriend, I hadn't seen much of her outside of school hours.

New buildings were appearing everywhere, mainly council flats to house the displaced families, along with new schools, as children still had to learn. Our area, which was close to the dockyards, was the worst bombed as this was where the shipyards and factories were.

I remember knowing about mother's friend during the war. Her work was something to do with intercepting secret messages sent by the enemy. She was stationed on an island off the coast but wasn't allowed to tell anyone where or when she was called to work. I hadn't told anyone, not even Alice, as I wasn't meant to know as I had been eavesdropping.

The war was a terrible time as we lost many people we knew, but most of all we lost John, not to war, but to his father who thought he had died in the bombing. He was lost to us forever it seemed and a little part of me died the day he was taken away. I wished he was still looking after me, even though I was now fifteen years old. Would I be like Alice and have had sex with him?

Even now the East End of London was still under construction all these years later. The government had done its best to house most of the poorer families who had no money. But there were still ruins to be torn down and the land rebuilt on. These activities were still reminders of the Blitz when there was so much destruction.

Alice's fate

Alice hadn't been to school for a couple of months and I missed her so much, so I decided to call at her home to see why she hadn't attended. Mother said I could visit her. For some reason, my curiosity got the better of me and just as I was about to leave, I asked Mother to tell me about sex. Well, she yelled and screamed at me, "Don't you even think about it. You get pregnant if you have sex, and you end up having a baby." I ran out the door and left her standing there yelling.

I had suspected this about babies, but it was still unsettling to hear it confirmed out loud. Did Alice know? As I walked to her place, I kept hearing what mother had said. Perhaps she was trying to scare me. I knocked on Alice's door and was greeted by her mother. "Is Alice alright? She hasn't been at school," I asked. Her mother stood with her hands on her hips. "Alice has gone; we sent her away." I was shocked; what did she mean? Where had my friend gone? It took a minute or two before I asked if I could visit her. "Did you know she was pregnant? We don't want her here living with us with a baby, so we sent her away. Goodbye, Beth," and with this the door closed. I froze in my footsteps. Oh my God, Alice with a baby; she was too young to be a mother.

As soon as I found a seat, I sat down and bawled my eyes out. This was the second friend I had lost. First John, now Alice!

Months ticked by and I missed my friend. Where was she, and how was she managing? I hoped she had been sent to a nice place to have her baby. Then one day some terrible news was circulating in the school grounds. A young girl's body had been found among some ruins, by children playing nearby. No one knew who it was. The police were still trying to find out who she was and where she may have lived. Was she a local or a stranger? My mind froze; this couldn't be Alice, surely not I told myself; she had been sent away, she hadn't run away. As the hours ticked by, no news was forthcoming, so I consoled myself that this wasn't my best friend.

The next morning there was a knock on our door. Mother was still in bed, so I answered it. There stood a policeman with a piece of paper in his hand. "Are you Beth?" he asked. When I nodded, he said, "As you may know, a young girl's body was found in the ruins recently. I'm very sorry to have to tell you the girl we found was Alice McMeeking. Her mother told us where you lived." He handed me a folded piece of paper. "This was found next to her body. It is addressed to you." I closed my eyes and prayed to God this was not true, but I knew it was. I would never see Alice ever again. "Was she your friend?" he asked. I nodded; no words would come out.

By this time my mother had come to the door. "What is going on?" she asked. The policeman told her a young pregnant girl had taken her own life and she had left a note for Beth. Before Mother thought about the situation, she turned on me. "Is that why you asked about sex? I told you what happened when you did that. Did you know Alice was having sex?" she asked. I nodded. I was in shock; my world was becoming a nightmare. With the note clutched in my hand I ran to my bedroom and lay on my bed howling. Like John, Alice was lost to me forever.

I opened the note to read: "Beth I'm sorry, I'll miss you. Don't have sex as you have babies. No one told me. My family told me to go, they didn't want me. Goodbye." I reread the note a hundred times trying to understand why she took her own life. I suppose she had nowhere to go. But her mother told me they had sent her away. I didn't think she had meant for it to end this way. But I hated her mother; if she had been kinder, I would still have Alice.

The days at school flew past as I dreamt about my absent friends. Mother still used me as a carer for my brother – some things never change – but I did notice Father was drifting apart from us. We hardly saw him and when he was at home, Mother yelled at him all the time. It wasn't long before he announced he was leaving our family. Mother flew into a rage and threw things at him. Now she would have to manage on her own. This spelled disaster.

The days came and went, and nothing changed; Mother was her usual selfish self. My brother looked upon me as his carer, and it was an escape when Father offered for us to come and visit him. He had a new lady friend and seemed really happy. She was nice to us and would sit and ask what we had been doing, which was new to us, as Mother never wanted to know about our lives. It was nice to see Father happy. He was a different man, and he did care about us children; he told us he loved us, but he couldn't live with Mother as she dragged him down and made him miserable.

Today I was starting my first job. I left school when I turned sixteen, and although Mother was not happy, I was. This was a release for me. I was working at a funeral parlour dusting and vacuuming for the first three months then they were going to teach me how to do fancy stitching, so I could help embroider the inside of the coffins. I couldn't wait to learn, as then I would know what had happened when Alice died. Her memory never left me as I thought of her every day. I remembered her words, "Don't have sex" so I made a promise to Alice and myself I was never going to do this until I was married and wanted to have a baby. At least I knew the consequences, but she didn't.

I met lots of people in my job, but most of the time they were sad as they had lost someone dear to them. I loved listening to the stories they told of the ones that had passed away. Then I understood it was okay to be sad, not always but some of the time. My brother was still at school, and he loved some of the stories I told him that came out of the funeral parlour.

Three months had passed, and I was now onto making the lining for the coffins. The materials were soft and delicate and mainly white, unless requested otherwise. It was important that everything looked beautiful as this was the deceased's last journey, before they disappeared. At this stage I had never been to a cemetery, so I didn't know what happened to the coffin once it left the parlour. In fact, I had never seen anyone in a coffin. That all happened in another room, which I was not privy to yet, because I was still a junior.

I did meet the young guy, Phil, who cleaned and polished the hearses. He kept all five of them immaculate as no one knew when they were needed, mainly because no one knew when they were going to die, it just happened ... like my friend Alice. Every time I passed the black cars I stopped and tried to see my reflection in the paintwork, as they were so shiny. One day I asked Phil what he used to clean them, and he told me, "Plenty of elbow grease." I thought that was a funny name to call a polish, but it certainly worked.

Phil and I talked a lot during our lunch breaks. He was a friendly guy and told me he was single. I sighed a breath of relief as I quite liked him. I didn't have to wait long before I was asked out on a date. He wanted to take me to the work 'do' as the funeral parlour was celebrating fifty years of trading. It was to be held in the reception room. The night had arrived, and I had bought a new dress to wear so felt quite smart. Mother was jealous of me going out so didn't wish me to have a pleasant evening.

As the night went on, people sipped or gulped away and lost control of their alcohol intake, then things started happening. Someone wheeled in a coffin and dared someone to climb inside. As I was the smallest person in the room all eyes turned to me. They lifted it on to the floor and all I had to do was climb inside and lie down. This I did, when suddenly a funny feeling overtook me: an unnatural calm. I wondered if this was how Alice felt before she was taken out to the hearse. My sadness disappeared as I thought that she would have been surrounded by beautiful soft fabrics, so clean and white … how peaceful.

As the night was nearing an end, Phil asked to walk me home, but it started to rain, in fact it was pouring. Our boss gave him the keys to a hearse to drive me home, providing he cleaned it the next morning, which was Sunday. This was my first ride in the shiny vehicle. We drove around until Phil found a lookout, so we pulled in and parked. Next thing he moved over beside me and started kissing me. It was full on, and I was trying to get my breath between kisses. Then I felt his hands touching my breasts. It felt nice so I didn't protest. But when he started to pull my knickers down, that's when I thought of my promise to Alice. "Phil, stop it. We hardly know each other," I reminded him. He was taken aback, perhaps thinking he was going to get his way with me, but this is where it ended. "Please take me home."

For the next few months Phil hardly gave me the time

of day. I had disappointed him, but I remembered my promise to myself and to Alice and that was more important. I loved my work as now they had hired a new junior, so I was full-time stitching and sewing the interiors of the coffins. Today my boss, Mr Atwell, asked if I would like to come into the next room and watch as they prepared a body. I hesitated; was I ready for this? I told myself I had to learn sooner or later so I agreed. I didn't last long in the embalming room, as it was all too much. I thought of Alice in that state and was overcome with grief.

That night as I lay in bed, I decided I needed to find a new job, something that made me happy instead of sad. I needed to laugh more. Also, Phil was dating the new junior; perhaps he was having sex with her.

I applied for a position in a pre-school, looking after children aged from eighteen months to five years, while their mothers worked, as many husbands didn't survive the war, which left the wives to provide for the family. This job was certainly a welcome change as I laughed every day while the kids were having fun.

A change of direction

As the years went by, I never thought much about dating, and I didn't have a chance to meet many boys. As I was heading home one afternoon, there was Phil standing outside the gate. I was surprised and wondered who was he here to see. As I punched my card into the slot to open the gate, he asked if he could talk to me in private. We walked for a bit, then he asked if he could take me out. I found I was still attracted to him, so I consented.

As time went by and we went out together, he did try to have sex with me, but I would never give in and told him it would be different when I was married and wanted a baby. This must have prompted him to propose to me, which he did. I said yes and before I knew it the big day had arrived. Mother didn't come to my wedding, but Father and his partner were there with my brother. It was a small affair as money was still scarce. Buildings were now dominating the skyline as things were moving towards normal at long last. It seemed like a lifetime since life was torn apart by war.

Phil and I lived in a rented prefabricated house that belonged to the funeral business. As it was associated with their firm, employees were allowed to rent it. I longed to leave home as Mother was becoming harder to bear, so this was the outlet I was waiting for. My brother had left home and was living with my father and his new partner.

Once I was married, it wouldn't matter if I had a baby, so now I could have sex. Phil was very patient during our courting days, but how that changed after we were married. Baby number one came within the first year, followed by baby number two, eleven months later. This brought back memories of John and how much he had helped out my mother when I was a baby. What had happened to him? Would I ever find out?

My days were filled with joy as I loved our kids. We had James then Sarah and now I was pregnant again; the last I told myself. It was at this time while pregnant that sad memories of Alice would haunt me. If only I could have helped her, but back then I was just fourteen, with no idea of grown-up life; I was still a child. But then, so was Alice. Who was this monster who had sex with her, knowing she could get pregnant? I remember her telling me that he was several years older than her and they had had sex lots of times. Surely being older, he would have known the consequences, which made her death all the more tragic.

Baby three was a difficult pregnancy. Her cries never rang out at birth, so a lot of slapping went on until a faint cough was heard. The nursing staff were rushing around, and the baby was taken away. At this stage I was so exhausted sleep overtook me, making my worries disappear. The next morning when I woke nursing staff were at my bedside, but no baby! "Where is my baby?" It was then I learned something was wrong and the doctor was on his way to speak with me. Tears fell from my eyes; what was I about to hear? I wished Phil was with me, but he was at home looking after our two children. What would he think?

I was disturbed by the doctor at my bedside. "Good morning, Mrs Rainer. I am here to break some sad news. Your little baby girl didn't get enough oxygen at birth. This was due to an umbilical cord prolapse. This means the umbilical leaves the cervix before the baby."

"What will happen to my baby, what does this mean?" I cried.

"It is too early to predict what effects it will have on her; we will just have to wait. She will have to stay in hospital for a few weeks as we do tests, but she will be well looked after," explained the doctor. I turned away from everyone and cried uncontrollably. Why did this happen to my baby, did I do something wrong? Was it my fault?" I sobbed. The doctor assured me I had done everything right. "Sometimes these unfortunate things happen for no apparent reason." Hearing these words made me feel a little better. "Would you like me to explain to your husband what has happened?" he asked. I thought about it but decided to tell him myself.

That night when Phil came to visit me, I tried to

explain to him but before I finished, he interrupted. "What does this mean? How will she be different to our other children?" I didn't know as I hadn't asked. "What do you mean you don't know? Surely you asked how different she would be to the other children. Really, Beth, sometimes I wonder what's in your head." Suddenly I saw another side to Phil, one that was alien to me. Why did he say this to me? Clearly, he knew I had been through a tough time, and I was as upset as him. "I'm off to find out what this baby will suffer, as well as what we will suffer. I don't want our life spoilt by a sick baby," he said as he left the room.

Two days passed before Phil came back to visit me. He still seemed upset. The ward sister told me what he had demanded from them, but like everyone else, he was told he would have to wait; no one knew what damage had been done at this stage. Tests were still being carried out. When I asked him to pick a name for our baby, he told me to sort it out. I knew from that moment he had put up a barrier between himself and this innocent little girl. It broke my heart to think there would be different feelings between our children, but it had already happened! He didn't stay for the full visiting hour. I felt hurt, and he probably felt betrayed.

The day finally arrived for Phil to pick up baby and me to take us home. He collected my bags and left me to carry Alice. "Why have you called her Alice?" he asked. I had thought hard about names and the one that meant so much to me was my friend Alice, who was always in my thoughts. By giving my baby this name, it would make her special to me. We now knew the test results. The impact of her birth misadventure would affect Alice's coordination, muscle control and balance, which in the future would compromise her independence, but that was years away I told myself. It didn't matter as we would all still love her.

James and Sarah loved their little sister, as there were no visible signs that she was different. It would only come to the fore when Alice was ready to sit. Phil had in his mind she was going to be a burden so didn't let himself get attached to her. I was disappointed that he took this attitude, as she was his daughter. But since her birth, things had not got back to being normal. Phil expected me to resume sex straight away, but it was the furthest thought from my mind as I didn't want any more babies. When I told him this, he was upset and told me I had a duty to please him. Sometimes I noticed he would stay away for the night, but this didn't worry me; I was left alone. His appetite for sex was too much and his demands left me cold.

One little question from Phil one day turned my whole world upside down. This was how it began: "Why did you call the baby Alice? I knew an Alice. I used to take her out, but one day she disappeared. I don't know what happened to her."

"Did she live in the Underground?" I asked. When he said yes, my heart missed a beat. Was this the same Alice I knew? Was Phil the older guy that she was having sex with? Surely not! I remembered a distinctive birthmark below her left eye, so I asked, "Did she have a birthmark on her face?"

"Yes, it was below one of her eyes. She was self-conscious about it, but it didn't worry me."

On hearing this I began to shake, and I was overcome with shame. It was then I realised I had married the very man who had got Alice pregnant, and worst of all, in my eyes he had caused her death. I couldn't help myself, but I had to know. "Did you have sex with her?" He proudly told me she was a virgin until they did it together. Before me stood a stranger, a person I didn't want to know as in my mind he was a murderer.

"What's wrong?" he said. "You weren't the first person I had sex with, so don't look so surprised." My knees felt weak and I had to sit down. I was dumbfounded and hurt to the very core. Suddenly a rush of adrenaline overtook me, and I had to let it out. "Alice was my best friend. She told me she was having sex with an older boy. I will tell you why she disappeared. She was pregnant and her family told her to leave home. What do you think happened to her?" Before Phil could answer I let fly. "She took her own life. Her body was found among the ruins by children who were playing nearby. Imagine how it affected them. The police brought a note to me that Alice had written. I'll tell you what it said: 'Don't have sex you get pregnant, no one told me'. Surely you knew the consequences of your actions, that girls could get pregnant. I hate you for that, Phil. You ruined a young girl's life."

Phil's answer made me feel sick. "Well, if they were

silly enough to have sex then it was their fault. I'm not responsible for them. I had fun. I remember Alice, though, she was cute." Now I hoped the shame would lie with him, but no, he had none!

For the next week I couldn't even bring myself to share the same bedroom, so I slept in Alice's room. Silence was the order of the following days, if not for the children's voices.

I had three children under four to care for, so the days came and went, and as promised Alice was my last baby. Although Phil tried to persuade me to have sex with him, the thought of what he had done to my best friend was too much for me. We acted like a normal family, but behind closed doors all was not rosy. Phil became angry because I would not please him, but I couldn't, as my love had turned to bitterness. He never once showed any remorse for what he did to Alice.

One day when Phil announced he had met someone else, it came as no surprise, and in fact it was a relief. It took several months for me to move into a council flat. Phil was still employed by the funeral home, so he was entitled to the house, meaning it was me and the children that had to leave. But I didn't want any reminders of him, so to move out was the only way of putting all this nightmare behind me. I could never forgive him for what had happened to Alice.

Two years passed, and I was a solo mother with three children. James and Sarah missed Phil. I didn't, and neither did Alice. He never had anything more to do with her; was it the name, or her disability? Whatever it was, she was an unwanted object to him. He was now settled with another partner, and they had James and Sarah every second weekend, which left me free to concentrate on Alice. She could only sit if propped up by cushions, as had been predicted by her doctor, as her balance was not good. But she learnt to crawl, and this was her means of getting around as balance didn't seem too much of a problem.

Six years on

Today was Alice's third visit to her specialist doctor. The hospital was keeping close tabs on her, as her stability had not got any worse since her first visit eighteen months ago. This was a plus, as it meant it wasn't deteriorating as she grew up. She was a happy little girl who had a very inquisitive mind, always asking questions. Her mode of transport was a special wheelchair that she could move herself, as she wanted to be independent. My father and his partner helped me buy her chair as I was struggling to make ends meet. Her brother and sister loved her and always fought over who was going to help her, but her independence won over most of the time. Her intelligence was above normal, which puzzled her teachers, but she was determined to succeed in life.

Phil never invited her to stay with him and his partner, even when the other two siblings asked. If only they knew the sorrow that was attached to Alice. He blamed her for their failed marriage, not admitting to himself that it might have been his fault.

Now that Alice was settled into school and enjoying her lessons, I was back looking after pre-schoolers at the university crèche, while mothers were furthering their education. This gave me the courage to look into finding myself something meaningful to study. If other mothers were doing it, why couldn't I? I wanted to help people, especially young girls who needed guidance in difficult times, when they had no one to turn to. There was still a lot of poverty and broken families, so Alice's scenario was probably happening every day to young girls that didn't have a mother figure to guide them in the right direction.

While working at the crèche I spoke with several mothers who were having problems of their own at home and didn't have anyone to talk to because of their heavy workload. This, along with memories of my friend Alice, helped me to decide where my path was going to lead me. Alice's pregnancy and death bugged me every day; it was like a burden I couldn't shake off, and along with this, it was a reminder of Phil, who I had never forgiven, as he had dismissed his association with Alice as a passing fling, and the result he had felt was not his worry, even though he got her pregnant. How callous was that? I hated him to the core, for his part in all this. I felt I had to warn young girls against predators like him, who had no concern for others and didn't accept any responsibility for their actions. To them it was a game: they were having fun and could walk away at any stage with no consequences.

So it was that I started on a new road. I first enrolled

in a community services course, with many more courses to follow. I juggled home life with study, making sure the family never suffered. Sarah and James were doing well at school, as was Alice. Her balance never got any worse, but it was just enough to compromise her ability to walk on her own, without aids. This didn't stop her bubbly personality shining through. My heart held a special place for Alice and although I loved my other two children, I'm not sure if it was her name that contributed to this feeling. Perhaps it was because Phil totally ignored her, and I overcompensated for his lack of affection.

Five years down the track, Sarah and James were both at university. Their visits to their father had almost become non-existent, as Phil had a new partner, which didn't come as a surprise, knowing his appetite for sex.

The next five years passed before my eyes in a flash, as all it comprised was family and study. First, I studied for a degree in psychology, then went on to social work, accompanying my children on school trips and holiday camps, which gave me hands-on experience working with children. This led me to a degree in human development and education. After this I finished a graduate degree programme in counselling to become a licensed counsellor. I would be my own boss and work hours that worked in with my children. I couldn't lose sight of the fact that Alice would always be my responsibility.

If not for my father helping me out financially, I would not have been able to achieve my dream. My mother had passed away which was a blessing, as she had become a burden on us all, expecting everyone to drop what they were doing to attend to her needs immediately. I asked myself what her purpose in life was but could not answer this satisfactorily, as she was never a capable mother. It was as if she hadn't found what she was looking for. I'm pleased Father found happiness with someone else. He always cared for my brother and me; it was just that he couldn't live with us because of Mother, but we both understood!

Alice was still making up her mind as to what career she would take up. She wanted to be independent, to be her own keeper, but I didn't know if she could achieve this on her own. Only time would tell. Meanwhile, she decided to go to university and get a degree in languages, as she felt it would open many doors. She had visions of travel, but I wondered if this would be possible as she would need someone with her. I let her believe in herself as she was a confident young woman, and I didn't want this to change. Her wheelchair was her lifeline to get to places, as this hid her balance disability. She looked perfectly normal; in fact she was attractive, with a personality that drew people to her, making her popular.

Where's Alice?

ONE EVENING after a night lecture at varsity, I received a call from Alice who called from the emergency phone in the student hallway to say she had missed the last bus. I told her to stay put in a highly lit area, by the spotlights at the front of the main building, and I would be there to pick her up in around thirty minutes. I panicked to think she was alone late at night in the varsity grounds, so I ran to the garage to start the car. For some unknown reason, the car wouldn't start. I tried several times to get it to go, but it wouldn't budge. I ran next door to my neighbour, and he came over only to discover I had a flat battery. He then drove his car over with a set of jumper leads to charge my battery, and suddenly away it went. All the time I was worried about Alice alone in the dark, as now nearly an hour had passed, and I still had to drive there. I sped through town looking out for traffic cops and thankfully there were none, so my journey was very quick.

When I reached the varsity, there was no sign of Alice. This is where I had told her to wait under the big lights, but as I looked everywhere there was no one in sight. Then I noticed something lying on the ground, so I went over only to find a briefcase that looked like hers. I picked it up and yes it was Alice's. Panic overtook me; where was she, had something happened to her? I screamed out her name over and over again, running everywhere, hoping she would answer me, but there was no response.

A police car went past so I tried to flag it down. It went a little further then backed back. An officer wound down the window and called out, "Are you alright, lady?" I ran up to the car screaming. "My daughter is missing. Please help me."

"What do you mean, missing?" he asked. I tried to tell them through my tears that I was meant to pick up my daughter, as she had missed the last bus. "I told her to wait under the spotlights until I arrived, but she is not here," I sobbed.

"Could she have gone off with a friend?"

"No, my daughter is in a wheelchair so she would have waited for me."

On hearing this the police looked concerned. They told me to sit in their car and they would call for backup. It was only a few minutes later that three more police cars arrived. "Please find my daughter," I said, sobbing uncontrollably. "Her name is Alice." The police formed a line, and they walked towards the back of the buildings to where there was dense woods. One of the officers stayed with me, asking questions about Alice. I clung to him as I had a bad feeling that something had happened to my daughter.

It wasn't long before a policeman came back with an item of clothing. "Do you recognise this?" he asked. I screamed, "That's Alice's jacket. Where is she?" It was then they realised this was a serious situation. Shortly after, the second item was retrieved; it was Alice's wheelchair, but no Alice. The police called for more backup and asked for a tracker dog. I don't remember much after that as I was taken to the police station, where a doctor was called to attend to me. He gave me a sedative and sat with me. All I could think of was my dear friend Alice. Did I do the wrong thing calling my daughter after her, was this tempting fate? Then I thought of Sarah and James; they would be at home wondering why I wasn't there. It was Phil's birthday, and he had invited them out for tea. "I must call my children and let them know what has happened," I explained to a police officer. She offered to drive me home, but my car was still at the varsity. "Don't worry, one of the officers will drop it off later. I will take you home now." The doctor gave me another couple of pills to take if I needed them, as I was complete mess

When James and Sarah saw me and the police officer at the door, they knew something had happened. "Mother, what's wrong?" Sarah said. I tried to answer but no words would come out, just sobs. The police officer explained as best she could. "Oh my God, what has happened to Alice? Will she be alright? Sarah asked. The officer said that they had a team of men and a dog handler searching the varsity grounds, at this very moment. James led me to the settee so I could sit down, then he put his arms around me. "It's okay, Mother. Alice is strong and she can handle herself." But when the children learnt Alice's jacket and her wheelchair had been recovered, the atmosphere changed from one of hope to one of helplessness. Now they joined me with sobs.

I don't know how I managed to sleep through the night, but I remembered taking the two pills, given to me by the doctor. It all seemed like a nightmare, but as I gathered my thoughts, it was still there. Where was my darling Alice? I dressed and made my way to the dining room only to find my two children consoling each other. When they saw me, they tried to hide their feelings, but pain was etched on their faces. "Mother, we have to be brave, that's what Alice would want," sobbed Sarah. "What could have happened to her?" asked James. "We had better let Father know." If I had my way I wouldn't have told him, but for the children it was the right thing to do. I asked James to ring Phil and let him know. I didn't want to speak with him.

Two more days passed, and all the police came up with was a shoe that belonged to Alice, but nothing else. The sniffer dog had picked up her scent, but suddenly it disappeared, pointing to the fact that Alice had been loaded into a vehicle and driven away. I was beside myself as now horrible thoughts had clouded my mind. The police were coming around to talk with us at five o'clock so James and Sarah had to be there. They did ask her father to attend, but upon informing him, he refused. This didn't surprise me as I knew his feelings regarding Alice. A long-forgotten thought came to my mind and that was of John. This was the longest period I had lost him from my thoughts but now he was back. Was this a comfort thing? Where was he and was he happy? I prayed his life was happier than mine at this moment.

The police arrived on time, and we all sat around the dining table. There they laid maps of the area they had searched and noted where Alice's belongings were found. Then one of the officers told us. "We are sorry to have to inform you, the conclusion we have come to is that Alice has been kidnapped and we are gravely worried for her safety. As each day passes there is less chance of finding her alive." This was my worst nightmare. I didn't want to hear these words; it was as if hope was fading.

"Who would have taken her? She was liked by everyone," I cried.

"We will be working on this case until it is solved. Sadly, there were no cameras focused on the woods area behind the university, but we can assure you that has changed, but it is of little comfort to you, I know. If there is anything we can do, just ask. In the meantime if you think of anything that might be of help, please contact us. If anything comes to light from our end, we will be in touch with you. Take care."

Now we all huddled together and prayed for a miracle to happen. We had to be strong and not let this destroy our family bond.

I took time out from work but managed to persuade

James and Sarah to continue at university. It was hard for them as they were at the crime scene each day and the students always wanted to know if Alice had been found. As the days passed, I didn't want to admit to myself that I didn't think I would ever see Alice again, but that thought lingered in my mind. My only hope was that she never suffered too much. My darling girl had left me forever, just like my best friend Alice. Thank God I still had John's memory to hang on to. He was with me more and more lately. "Please God let him be safe," I muttered to myself.

My father and his partner were a great help to me, as was my brother. They put funds together to buy me a small office of my own to take my mind away from Alice. The children told me Phil's latest partner had left him. This had happened before his birthday, which is why he had asked them out for dinner, as he didn't want to celebrate on his own. Apparently, he was not good company. Life had let him down, so they left early to allow him to wallow in his own self-pity. He had asked them to visit more regularly, and he had even asked after me, not that I cared!

My little business was picking up as clients were being referred to me by the schools I had visited, which was good as now I had to concentrate on other people's problems and forget mine. James and Sarah had been discussing going overseas together, as the loss of Alice had brought them closer together. They decided to have time out from studies for one year. They worried about me, but I was busy so encouraged them to go, as it would take their young minds off what was happening here.

"Why don't you and Father get together?" James asked. "You are both on your own."

What could I say? Just the thought of sharing a space with Phil made me cringe, as in my mind he was my friend Alice's murderer. "Why didn't Father have anything to do with Alice? Was she not his child? Did you have an affair?" he continued. This stirred me up. Fancy thinking I was the culprit in all this. "Sarah and I have talked about this many times, so now I am asking." I thought for a moment; I didn't want to destroy their relationship with their father, but now was the time to explain my side of the story.

After they had both listened to my account, Sarah put her arms around me and cried. She, being a female, understood feelings more than James. Both were upset with their father, but now understood he was Alice's biological father. They realised there was nothing left to salvage in our marriage ... it was dead and buried.

They had one more visit to their father before leaving on their overseas trip. While away if anything came to light on Alice's disappearance, they were to be informed immediately. Deep down we all knew she was not coming back to us, but no one wanted to make it final. The police were at a stalemate as there were no clues, but the case was far from closed.

The children's last visit to their father before leaving was anything but pleasant. He asked them to try to persuade me to have him back, but when he knew the children had been told about his past, he was livid.

"Why did you not like Alice?" Sarah asked her father.

"She was the cause of our marriage breakdown; your mother should never have given her that name."

Sarah couldn't understand what the name had to do with anything. "But Father, you can't blame a child for that. She was your daughter. Poor Alice. I will always love and remember her. She was a sweet girl. You missed out on so much; what do you feel now that she has disappeared?"

Phil just brushed this question off but did mutter under his breath, "She was the one that destroyed us. Your mother chose her over me." This answer was not what they expected, as it soured the whole evening, bringing it to an abrupt end. Sarah never wanted to see her father again. She was pleased she and James were leaving for overseas. James had listened and was not impressed. He felt disappointed with his father.

Feeling alive again

Now with the children gone, something was missing from my life. My sexual feelings were non-existent, as I had given my heart to the wrong man. I remember reading one day , 'Never give the key to your heart to anyone. Always keep it with yourself'. How I wished I had followed that advice. My self-esteem was low so I decided to join a meditation class for four sessions, to see if I could find myself again. I desperately needed my mojo back. All my life comprised was work, taking on other people's problems, but then, I did want to help people, so this was part of what I chose to do. But I had forgotten about myself and my problems, yet I was the one who needed help! Perhaps meditation was the answer!

The police were still in touch, as they didn't like having an unsolved missing person's case, which had now been upgraded to one of murder. Finding the wheelchair was the deciding factor, as Alice could not survive without it;

it was her lifeline. Later the police were going to visit me and introduce me to a new recruit, a detective, Tobias Metcalf, who had familiarised himself with the case and would work on it as his sole project. He could not accept there were no answers, so he set out to prove someone must have seen something that night.

After lunch the police called at my office and introduced me to Metcalf. He seemed very young, not at ease with himself, almost shy and awkward. He asked if he could make an appointment to spend a couple of hours with me at home, away from work, where we could talk uninterrupted. This was arranged for the next Saturday as my office would be closed. He shook my hand with a firm grip as he left. This proved to me he was not as weak as I might have first thought.

Come Saturday, Metcalf was right on time, accompanied with his briefcase full of papers. We sat down at the dining-room table so he could lay everything out in order. I noticed he was quite meticulous with his paperwork. He started by asking me about my personal life so he could paint a picture in his mind. I didn't go into details as to why I was no longer with my husband, as I felt this was irrelevant. An hour later he had all the details he needed to proceed with the case.

"Did you know of anyone who might have wanted to harm Alice, any acquaintances or friends?" I told him Alice was well liked by all who knew her, as she was a girl who did not let her disability stop her from enjoying life. Then the conversation came to the night she disappeared. I told him word for word what happened that night, how the car battery was flat and that had held me up an extra hour.

"Where were her siblings?" he asked. I told him they were at their father's, as it was his birthday. "Did Alice get on well with them?" I told him they both loved her. "What about her father, was he close to her?" I hesitated; what could I say without being bitter, and I didn't really want that side of my life exposed. "No, they weren't on speaking terms."

"Why was that?" he asked.

"Could we just skip that in the meantime? That's another whole story," I answered. He could see that I was upset and said we would come back to it at a later date.

"Can I have a look around the house, with you accompanying me to Alice's bedroom?"

I showed him to Alice's room where he walked around and touched a couple of her items. It was left exactly as it was the day Alice disappeared. "Do you have any recent photos of her?" The most recent one was on the dresser in my bedroom, the photo I kissed every night before getting into bed. "I can't let this one go. I couldn't live without it," I sobbed. All the time I tried to be brave, but eventually I broke down.

"I'm so sorry, may I call you Beth? It must be heartbreaking not to know what happened to Alice, and you are very brave." With this he took my arm and led me back to the dining room.

"Thank you, Mr Metcalf, for being patient with me. I try to be brave, but every now and then it becomes too much for me," I sobbed.

"Please call me Toby. This is a terrible burden on you, but you're doing just great. I will go now, but if I need any further information, I will be in touch. Goodbye for now, Beth, and thank you." On leaving, he took my hand in his and lay the other hand on top. Suddenly, my body felt alive. I had never encountered this feeling in my life, so why now?

Sunday was my meditation group; this was my third session, and I was loving it. Sadly, we only had one more session, then it was up to each of us to carry on with it, in our own time. I set myself half an hour first thing each morning before breakfast, to meditate on my own. This was my time. I could not believe the difference I felt about myself. It was amazing; my self-belief and self-confidence were returning. This had all disappeared after learning about my best friend, and the part Phil had played in this nightmare. Also, I was missing John and, most of all, my darling daughter Alice. I didn't know how much I was lost to myself.

At work on Monday, I received a call from Toby requesting to call and see me at my office at five o'clock. He said he had a new lead; well, a bit of information that might be handy, but he wanted to talk to me. Just hearing his voice sent shivers down my spine. What was happening to me? I was like a teenager on a first date.

As I was saying goodbye to my last client for the day, Toby arrived. It seemed strange calling him Toby especially as Tobias sounded quite proper. I invited him in, and we sat down at my desk. He stated, "I have been out calling on all the residents who live in the vicinity of the university and uncovered what I think might be a clue. Someone saw a black hearse late that night, just past the woods area of the university. At this stage I don't know if this is relevant, but it has given us something to work on, I just wanted to let you know. I will visit all the funeral parlours in the vicinity, then in the city, even venturing further afield."

Toby was like a dog with a bone, but this was his job, and I began to think he was good at it. When saying goodbye, he shook my hand. I didn't want to let go as those strange intimate feelings were flowing through my body. I felt alive and excited! But alas, he had to carry on, as this was a business call, I had to remind myself.

Meditation became an important part of my life, as did my appearance. I was now looking in the mirror to see where improvements could be made. It seemed years since I took any notice of how I looked, and my past hadn't given me any reason to take hold of myself, but how that had all changed since Toby had come on the scene. I felt a new person, and feelings that were dormant for years were making themselves known to me and I was loving it. But I had to remind myself of the age difference, as Toby was youngish and I was older. It didn't seem right … but I was just Beth to him, a sort of client!

Tonight, I received a call from James and Sarah who both tried to talk to me over one another. I had to tell them, "One at a time." They were having a wonderful time. "Has there been any news of Alice? We think of her every day," said Sarah. James was pleased when I told him there was a new detective on the case, solely to solve

Alice's disappearance. They were picking up work along the way, so their finances were holding up fine.

"Mother, we are working our way to Peru to visit Machu Picchu. It will take us about three months, but I am telling you now as we both want you to meet us there. We know this is a place you have always talked about. We are giving you plenty of time, so please think about it." Yes, Sarah was right, it was one of my dream places to visit, but that was a long time ago. Although since beginning meditation, I had that inkling back. I could imagine myself sitting on the citadel's stone walls in the lotus position, watching the mist as it made its way over the mountain tops and curled itself around the terraces.

"Yes, Sarah. I will meet you and James there in three months' time. Count me in." We talked on for several minutes, then the phone cut out.

Another person's problems

Today was a sad reminder of my past. A young girl, Sally, just thirteen years of age, found out she was pregnant, so came to my office wanting help. She didn't know where to go or who to tell. She had lost her parents to the war and was living with an uncle and aunt. I started by asking how old the father was, thinking it was a school friend. When she said he was a middle-aged man, my heart sank. Was this a fleeting affair; did she know the man? With this, she burst into tears. "I didn't want to do it, but he made me. He told me he would tell my aunty that I beg him for sex; what could I do?" My stomach churned when I heard this. It was his own niece; only an animal would do such a thing.

"Do you want to keep the baby?" I asked.

She didn't want to as it would always remind her of this sordid part of her life, one she wanted to forget. "I can't tell my aunt as she has been so good to me," she sobbed.

This situation had to be resolved, and her uncle had to face some consequences for his selfish actions. He would not get away scot free, I would make sure of it! I knew from experience the sad crushing results that can come from these situations, but thank goodness she had come for help. I needed time to think how to handle it all so asked her to come back on Friday. She left her phone number with me.

On my way home I called into the police station to see if there was any update on Alice's disappearance. I was shown to Toby's office, only to find him sitting in his chair behind a tidy pile of papers neatly placed in order. He greeted me and asked me to sit down.

"I am still frantically working with all the funeral parlours to find out if any of them may have had a hearse on the road that particular night, but so far there are no results. But I'm not finished yet. I won't give up until I have questioned every goddamn one.

"At one of the local parlours I visited, a man wanted to know why I was wanting information, and he seemed uneasy but assured me they didn't have a hearse on the road that night.

"Are you on your way home? Would you like a ride?"

I accepted, as any contact with Toby made me feel great; he was like a miracle pill. On the way we chatted about everyday life, and it was only when we pulled up at my driveway that it occurred to me to mention the visit from the young teenager. I would not have talked to anyone else other than Toby, because it was confidential, but I thought he might think soundly on this subject. He was saddened by what I told him, and yes, the perpetrator had to be punished. The uncle had ruined a young girl's life. He was her guardian, someone who was meant to protect her, not harm her, and he had committed a grave injustice, so the result would likely be prison.

"How do I advise her? She doesn't want to keep the baby, which is probably the sensible decision, but an abortion must be her decision. I can't influence her in any way; it has to be her choice. Then there's the aunty; how is she going to take this? It makes me sick when an act of sexual violence is forced upon anyone, but a thirteen-year-old, that is despicable."

Toby listened and took everything in. Maybe he sensed that something had gone awry in my life too.

"Perhaps you should ask the girl to bring her aunty along to your next meeting, then you can both break the news. She might even want to keep the baby."

I thanked Toby for his input, as it was good to run this past someone else. He alighted from the police car and walked around and opened my door.

"You're a gentleman as well," I said.

He reached over and helped me out. For a moment I imagined myself in his arms, and a fleeting romantic feeling ran through my body, only to abruptly come to an end. As he drove off, I stood and wrapped my arms around myself. I felt on a high, but gravity soon brought me back to earth.

Breaking the news

From my office, I called Sally on her home phone and asked how she felt about bringing her aunt to my office, then I could help her break the news. I would be there to protect her if her aunty retaliated in any way. Sally felt sick having to tell her about her husband, and she knew her aunt would be in denial.

"But, Sally, your uncle forced himself on you. He is an animal, and she has to know. I will protect you if there is any backlash. It will be better to do it this way, as I will be your witness."

Finally, she agreed.

Friday arrived and I was prepared for whatever was about to happen when Sally walked in for her appointment. As she sat down, she introduced me to her aunt. I was surprised, as she was a very modern-looking woman, well dressed and very attractive. What would make her husband go outside their marriage for sex? Was it the fantasy of conquering a virgin? My thoughts were disrupted when the aunt asked why she was here. I looked at Sally and the tears started. She nodded to me to begin.

"This is going to be a shock for you, but Sally is pregnant..." Before I could say anything else the aunt interrupted. "I have talked to you about sex, Sally. You knew the consequences, but you are just a child. Who is the father? Is it one of the lads from school?" Sally's tears began to flow uncontrollably. I went around and held her hand. Now it was time to tell the truth. "Will you tell who the father is, or do you want me to say?" I asked. With this she spat out, "Uncle Rob."

It was as if lightning had struck. The aunt went into overdrive. "Don't be silly; why blame your uncle? He loves you. He is a good man." This is where I intervened. "Sally is telling the truth. Your husband, her uncle, took her against her will, in fact he forced himself upon her, which is punishable by a stint in prison. I'm sorry you had to hear this, but you had to know. He cannot carry on with his unsavoury behaviour; it has to finish right here. Sally will come back to my home tonight, while you deal with your husband. The police will be at your place tomorrow morning to take him away."

"I'm sorry, Aunty," sobbed Sally. Her aunt got out of her chair and looked at Sally in disbelief. Her parting words were, "If this is true, I will kill him." There was still no discussion or decision about the baby.

Sally and I went to a takeaway outlet and bought some

food to have at home. Tonight she was going to be away from the man who had taken advantage of her. Now it was her aunt who had to deal with him. After we had eaten, we sat and talked.

"What am I going to do about the baby?" Sally asked.

"The decision is yours alone, Sally. What are you thinking?"

"I think an abortion is the only solution, as then I can go back to school and finish my education. I'll only be off school for a week; no one need know why."

I agreed. She had her whole life ahead of her. This was a setback, but hopefully she could put it all behind her and move forward. She said she was tired and wanted to go to bed. I took her to Alice's room and took a nightdress from a drawer. This was the first time the room had been used since Alice's disappearance. "Whose room is this?" Sally asked. I told her it belonged to my daughter Alice. Of course, she asked where Alice was. I sat on the bed with Sally and told her Alice's story to date, which brought more tears. I hugged her, thinking for one long moment that I had Alice in my arms.

I drove to work the next morning, stopping off at the police station. After speaking with Toby, a police car was sent around to Sally's aunt's house to arrest her husband. Sally had been still sound asleep when I left, so I let her sleep on. When I arrived at work Sally's aunt was waiting for me.

"I'm here to apologise for yesterday. It came as a shock. How is Sally?" I asked her to come into my office. We sat down and talked about Sally's future. She and Sally had both made the same decision on the baby, unbeknown to each other. I would arrange the abortion with the right persons the following Tuesday, then life could return to near normal for Sally. Her aunt wanted her to come back and live with her, now that the uncle was gone.

The search goes on

ONE MONTH ON, Toby turned up at my office to say he had had no luck with his enquiries, as he had found no one who had a hearse on the road that fateful night. He was now concentrating on the jacket and the wheelchair to see if he could recover any DNA. These items were locked away in a special evidence room housed at the back of the main police station. This was the beginning of using DNA as a source of identification in murder cases. Toby explained it had recently begun in the UK and had only been used a few times, it was still in its infancy, but was proving to be a vital source for incriminating evidence, especially in an unsolved murder.

"Did Alice know of anyone who might have been linked to a funeral parlour?" Toby asked. For a moment I was speechless; had I not told Toby her father worked for an undertaker? But Phil? Surely he would never hurt his own daughter. Then I thought back to what had happened to my best friend and doubts started to creep in. I reminded myself this was only my interpretation of the cause of Alice's death. Phil had used her for sex, but it was Alice who took her own life, and it was me who branded him as a murderer, because of him getting her pregnant. Her family had cast her aside, so this was another nail in her coffin, something I still hadn't forgiven them for.

"Alice's father works for a local funeral director. He has been there for years, that's where I met him. I should have told you earlier, but I didn't think it was important." I watched as Toby got out his notebook. "You said he didn't have anything to do with Alice; why?" At that moment my next client arrived, so I asked Toby to come by my house later and I would explain the situation. He stood up and said he would see me around 7.30. We shook hands and that feeling of closeness passed through my body once again. Any contact with him left a warmth that was unexplainable. I had to remind myself I was much older than him, but did that really matter?

I left my office a little earlier to make sure the house was tidy when Toby arrived. I even found time for a shower and to put on a nice dress. I felt like an excited schoolgirl. "For heaven's sake, Beth," I scolded myself, "this is a business meeting not a social affair!" Was this because I wanted it to be more of an intimate exchange? I had to remind myself he was coming to talk about Alice; why was I thinking of myself instead of my daughter? But this did little to quash my feelings.

I heard the doorbell ring, so looked at my clock only to find it was seven o'clock. My heart raced. He was early;

was this a sign? On opening the door, there stood Phil. My joy turned to disappointment. "What are you doing here?" I asked, still in shock. I told him I had a visitor coming at 7.30, and he would have to leave before then.

"I'm worried. I haven't heard from James and Sarah. Have they contacted you?" I told him they had called several times and were having a great time.

"I'm very disappointed they haven't called me. Could you tell them next time they call I would like to talk to them?"

What could I say? Even though I knew why, I didn't want to become involved. We stood looking blankly at each other. It was Phil who broke the silence. "I hear you are doing well; how did you afford an office and this house?" he quizzed. This was none of his business I told myself.

He didn't enquire about Alice's disappearance, which told me he was the same old Phil, and nothing had changed! I asked him if he still worked for the same funeral parlour, and he said he did. I presumed he still lived in the rented house, but didn't ask, as his life meant nothing to me. My body tensed in his presence, and all I could think of was my friend Alice and how tragically her life had ended. I looked at the clock to see it was nearly 7.30, so I asked Phil to leave.

As I opened the door, there stood Toby about to ring the bell. I panicked as I didn't want them to meet, but it was too late. "Hi Toby, Phil is just leaving. He is my ex. Bye, Phil," I said as I asked Toby to come in.

"I've met you, haven't I?" Toby said to Phil. "Yes, I

remember I met you at a funeral parlour. You were the man I spoke to about the hearse being out late the night Alice went missing."

Phil was taken by surprise, and this showed on his face, which turned scarlet, and his gaze dropped to the ground. "Did you talk to Phil's boss?" I asked. This was to make it quite clear that he was just an employee.

"When I asked to speak to someone in charge, he said he would handle it, so that's what happened," said Toby. With this, Phil scurried off.

Once settled at the dining-room table, Toby took out his journal and pen. "I'm still unclear as to why your ex didn't have anything to do with Alice. Can you enlighten me as to why this was so?" he asked. Where would I start? There was only one place and that was right at the beginning, back with my friend Alice's suicide, then what followed from there. He jotted down points of interest as I rambled on. I was on a hate journey brought to the fore by Phil's unexpected visit today.

When I eventually stopped, I apologised for my prolonged babble. I felt I needed to let it all out. My frustrations had been building up over weeks and when I realised this, the tears followed. "Beth, are you okay? Do you want me to go?" Toby asked as he stood up. I felt a fool; I didn't want to break down in his company. I apologised and asked him to stay. It took all my strength to restrain myself from letting my feelings known to him. The first move had to be made by Toby, as I didn't know if this was a one-sided attraction.

"When I see Phil, he leaves me in a mood that I find

hard to explain. It is anything but happy, and in fact I feel detached from life. What I saw in him makes me question my judgement of men. But I was young, wanting to get away from my mother for a more stable life, then Phil came along and filled that void. He was the only boyfriend I had ever had. When the children came along, I was happy. That was until I discovered his past, then everything soured. It was his attitude and no showing of remorse for what happened to my friend Alice that was the last straw. I'm sorry for boring you with my life's history, Toby."

"It is good to let it all out, Beth, and sometimes it helps to have someone to listen. You are under a lot of stress. I think you are very brave, so you don't have to apologise to me."

Just hearing these comforting words made my heart race and a warmth enveloped me … if only … but I couldn't, I was the older woman. If anything was to happen it would be at Toby's initiative, this privilege was his … not mine.

The days went by, and I was kept busy trying to help others solve their problems. I loved my work, and if I could make one person a day happy, I felt I was doing my job well.

Sally called in. She had had her abortion and was back at school. No one knew of her setback; this was between her aunt, herself and me. The uncle admitted to his sins, so it meant Sally didn't have to attend a trial, thus sparing her any ongoing agony. The aunt would never entertain the idea of taking her husband back; he was history.

I had a call from James and Sarah, who were still having a wonderful time. They called to remind me I only had four weeks to book my airfare to Peru, so a date was settled on, and all the rest of the arrangements would be made by them. All I had to do was meet them at the airport.

I told them to call their father as he was concerned that they hadn't been in contact with him. "I will leave that to James, as I haven't forgiven him for ignoring Alice all those years. Fancy him shunning her when she was his child," said an angry Sarah.

It was the right time to tell them that Toby was now working on DNA traces on the recovered items, as the hearse avenue had reached a stalemate. They were happy to know the case was still being investigated and that it hadn't been forgotten as time passed. "Phil and I had to give DNA samples, as family are always the starting point of elimination for a family disappearance or murder," I told them both.

Two weeks later, Toby was coming to see me to ask questions about Phil. He didn't want to speak to me during working hours, so arranged to meet me at my home. My heart was racing hearing his voice again. I had missed his presence but couldn't think of an excuse to turn up at the police station. He was constantly on my mind, and when I felt a little down, I only had to think of him, which enabled warmth to flow through my body and bring happiness back ... I could live with that! Then I had to remind myself that to Toby I was an older client. Although a glimmer of hope was there, because sometimes when our eyes met, I felt there was a glint of something special between us. Was I reading too much into this? If so, that was okay!

As Toby opened his briefcase and put his papers on the table, I offered him an alcoholic drink, but he declined, as he was here on case work. I had not seen him quite so business-like. "Please sit down, Beth, I have some questions I hope you can help me with. DNA from Alice's wheelchair was analysed and there is a match with Phil's DNA. Can you throw some light on this?"

I was shocked; how could this be? I had to think: were we still together when Alice got her wheelchair? My mind was all over the place; that was years ago, so how was I meant to remember? "It was over sixteen years ago when she got her wheelchair, was Phil still around? How could DNA still be on the wheelchair?"

Toby suddenly became the efficient detective. "Beth, Alice's wheelchair has been in police storage since her disappearance. There will be other fingerprints, but at this moment we have a match to Phil's. What we have to establish is how did his DNA come in contact with Alice's chair?" I had to think back again as to what age Alice was exactly when we bought her wheelchair. She had it before she started school. Phil was not present in our lives at that time. I didn't remember him ever being near her wheelchair.

Toby appeared to be in deep thought; his pen was tapping the table, and his gaze was fixed out the window. As I looked at him, I could see he was definitely processing something. I wished it was about me. "Are you sure you won't have a drink?" I asked again. This time he nodded and seemed to snap out of wherever he was. I poured two glasses of chardonnay, one of which I sat on the table in front of him. We were going to relax a little and talk about something other than Alice's case.

I told him about my intended trip to Machu Picchu. Toby listened as I explained my plans. He broke my concentration by saying he and his wife had visited several years back. This was the first mention of a wife, but I knew deep down in my heart that he wouldn't be unattached. If I had feelings for him, surely, I wouldn't be the only one. A flash of sadness crossed my mind, so I told myself dreams were free; they didn't hurt anyone. But I still felt there was a little flicker of something when our eyes met; it was as if he knew my feelings. If that was all of him I could have, I could live with that, but this wasn't the first time I had told myself this.

I asked him to tell me all about Machu Picchu. He became very enthusiastic as he explained the overwhelming effect it had on him. It had given him a new perspective on life, as he had never really thought about the spiritual realm until his visit, but it had changed his way of thinking. As he spoke, his hands were crossed on his heart; was he still there in the Andes? I was mesmerised: was it because of his story, or was it my heart that was aching for him?

"You will love it Beth. It was fantastic but describing it doesn't do it any justice. To be there and experience it, it catches the very essence, and when the mist gently appears over the mountains and floats down the valley, that is so surreal. Prepare yourself for a wondrous adventure. I can imagine you there; you will love it."

These words nearly brought tears, not just a couple, but bucketloads. I quickly picked up my glass and took a couple of rather large sips to prevent any unwanted words flowing out, ones I would later regret!

"I want to talk to you again before you leave for Peru. If you can remember roughly the date that you and Phil parted, if it was before or after you bought Alice's wheelchair. Please call me before you go. Have a wonderful time, Beth, you deserve it." He held out his hand to shake mine as he was leaving, and I did the unthinkable, while shaking my hand I held on to his longer than was normal, and our eyes met, He smiled as if in acknowledgment of my feelings. My heart was racing, and I felt a flushing feeling overtaking me. Did he notice? By the time I gathered my thoughts, Toby was getting into his car.

As I was getting ready for bed, my thoughts were back with Toby. I remembered he asked when Phil and I had parted. I had to think back to when we purchased the wheelchair. Suddenly it all came to me: my father had helped me buy the chair as I was on my own, and Phil was well gone. It was too late to call Toby so I would have to leave it until the morning. His image was still in my mind when I climbed into bed and cuddled into my pillow, thinking it was his body lying with me, sharing my bed.

Embarrassed by my lingering handshake, I elected to call Toby, so I didn't have to come face to face with him. I let him know that Phil had left us before the wheelchair was purchased. I wasn't sure how this would help him with Alice's investigation, but I had supplied the information he asked for. It was only a couple of days until I was off on my journey, and I was looking forward to catching up with James and Sarah, but sad to be leaving Toby.

Machu Picchu, here I come

WHEN THE PLANE landed at Anta airport, I was relieved to feel the wheels hit the runway, as this was the longest flight I had ever taken. I couldn't wait to see my children again; my excitement was building. As I entered the terminal hundreds of people were making their way through customs, so it was just a matter of following the leader. Forty minutes later I emerged from the arrival area into the arms of Sarah, who was shedding tears as we hugged each other. James picked up my luggage and waited for his turn for a hug. Our accommodation was near the airport, so we flagged down a taxi. As I studied James, I couldn't see any likeness between him and Phil, which pleased me no end, as I didn't want any reminders.

Once we were settled into our hotel, talk flowed as I learnt of all the places they had visited and what a wonderful time they were having. Then our conversation switched to Alice. I couldn't tell them any more than what they already knew, as nothing new had come up. I did say that Toby was following up on the DNA aspect and he would let me know if anything came to light, as he knew the pain I carried in my heart.

The day had come for us to catch the train up to Machu Picchu. I was full of excitement and enthusiasm, as I knew, with how Toby had described it, that I wanted to experience the same feelings. We were leaving from Ollantaytambo where we were taking the ninety-minute train ride to the gateway town of Aguas Calientes. On our arrival we had a choice of a twenty-minute bus ride or a two-hour walk. James and Sarah fancied the walk, but not me. I wanted to get there the quickest way possible, so arranged to meet them amid the ruins, somewhere.

We said our goodbyes as I boarded the bus. This gave me time to think of Toby; was he remembering that I was on a journey of self-discovery, a journey of connection of both our spirits? Was this wishful thinking that our spirits might one day join together? Wrong or right, this thought warmed my heart.

"Ladies and gentlemen, we have arrived at our destination. You are visiting a place steeped in history and mystery. Please disembark. You will find all the information you need inside the main entrance of this historic sanctuary." Suddenly my mind reconnected with my body, and dreamtime was over. As I stepped from the bus and walked towards the entrance, there before me stood breathtaking vistas of terraced hills, stone ruins and mist-shrouded peaks. The sheer beauty of the Andes enveloped me. I was here, witnessing the silent reverence of this place, a place where nature, history and spirituality converged.

I was happy I was on my own, as I wanted to feel the energy emanating from the sanctuary of this sacred land, be it real or imagined. At the moment my imagination was running wild; in fact, it was uncontrollable. Nothing I had ever seen came anywhere near what was before me, and it left me speechless and breathless. I walked to the nearest stone structure and let my hands feel the roughness of the ruins, and a feeling of connection overcame me.

I was taken back to the past, where this civilisation first began centuries ago. Whatever happened to the Incan people, why did they disappear and leave behind these monumental ruins? Were they taken out by a deadly plague of smallpox, or was there an invasion? One's mind was left to wonder what really happened ... no one knows exactly even to this day.

I walked to one of the terraces and sat down on my pack in the lotus position to see what thoughts came to me. The moment I closed my eyes silence overcame me, and the stillness brought on a peacefulness that absorbed all my thoughts. My mind was empty. What was happening? This was all new to me, and suddenly a warm feeling came from my heart and an energy was emerging, filling me with complete happiness. Was this a spiritual experience? If so, then I knew something wonderful had happened. If I meditated here, could I feel the same happiness with future meditations back home? There was only one way to find out!

When I felt someone touching my arm, I opened my

eyes in surprise. "Mother, are you okay? You were asleep," laughed James. This was the end of my meditation. "Isn't this incredible? It would have to be the most moving place we have visited. This is such a spiritual place, look at the mist, hanging around the mountains as if it is guarding this whole sacred valley. It is keeping the evil spirits out."

"Oh James, I'm so happy you feel the spiritual vibe. I thought it was just me. I will never forget this place; it will be with me forever. It is sad that something so special was just abandoned. Whatever happened to the Incan people … where did they go?"

"No one knows, Mother. It is a mystery probably never to be solved, but that is why this place has such a presence. It is surrounded by a mystical beauty, and it is like stepping into a time capsule. Let's take a walk and enjoy it together."

Sarah was very quiet. Like me, she found it overwhelming, but didn't need to speak, as it was all there in front of her. Was this a female thing? Although there were busloads of visitors, there was a quiet reverence, and only whispers could be heard.

As we walked along the terraces, we saw different aspects of this sanctuary. We climbed steps and came across a semi-circular construction built over an enormous rock, which was known as the Temple of the Sun. This was a place where Incan priests worshipped the sun. Our view from up here was breathtaking: the ruins stood out in their neat terraces, as did the background of mountains and bush-clad inclines, then far below in the valley was the river. The mist was descending upon the mountains as it was getting late, and a gong rang out, letting us know it was time to return to the bus.

Our time at Macha Picchu was over, but the memories will live on, never to be forgotten. All too soon we were back on the bus, leaving behind a place that will be cemented in my mind and heart forever! Oh, Toby, how right you were, when you said words couldn't do it justice. It had to be seen to be believed, and even then it was almost unbelievable!

Toby's breakthrough

HERE I WAS BACK at home, but a little part of me was left behind at Machu Picchu. Each morning when I meditated, it meant so much more, as I felt a strange spirit had come back with me, to guide me in my everyday life. I felt more spiritually connected, which brought joy and happiness within, closing out negativity and inviting in positivity. My life was changing, but not for one moment did I forget my darling Alice.

I hadn't let Toby know I was back as I needed time to think and reflect. Today was the day to contact Toby, but before I called him, he called me.

"Hi Beth, how did it all go? Did I do it justice when explaining, or did I not? You have to experience it for yourself to feel the spiritual sensations, so now you will know what I meant. I called to say we have a lead in Alice's disappearance. It is too early to say anything at the moment, but as soon as we are 100 per cent sure I will let you know. Call in and see me if you are passing, as I would love to hear your story. Bye for now."

I knew in my heart there was going to be a breakthrough in Alice's case, not today but in the near future. Toby must have been working on it and discovered something that was of importance, but why couldn't he tell me? Perhaps if I called in at his office tomorrow on my way to work, I might be able to persuade him to tell me what they had found. I knew within my heart Alice was not alive, but what had happened, and why? It would have been delusional if I had any thoughts of Alice still being here with us. As time went by and with no clues as to where she might be, hope was vanishing. I struggled, thinking of the worst scenario.

I arrived at the police station and asked to see Toby. The person behind the reception desk told me he had been called away unexpectedly, and they couldn't say when he would be back. "I hope it is nothing serious?" I enquired, hoping there would be a clue forthcoming, but no, this was the police after all … nothing disclosed! I walked out feeling deflated. I hoped nothing had gone wrong in his personal life. Just as well I had a busy day in front of me, as it would take my mind away from Toby, but I did wonder what lead he had on Alice's disappearance.

The day went by fast, contrary to how I thought it would play out. My clients' problems were solvable, and it was one of my better days. I could go home and relax; tomorrow was another day!

As I was sipping my wine, the phone rang. "Hello,

Beth, it's Toby here. Are you home on your own? Can I come over?" My heart started racing; he wanted to visit, and of course that was okay. He didn't have to ask but I said yes.

After getting off the phone I ran to my bedroom and slipped into a nice dress, put on some make-up and lastly a spray of perfume ... job done. "Play it cool, Beth" I told myself, hoping to control my temperature and not end up with cheeks the colour of a beetroot. I sat down and sipped my wine, pretending to be in complete control. When the doorbell rang, up I jumped and almost ran to the door.

"Hello Toby, come in," then we made our way to the lounge. "First, tell me about Machu Picchu. Did it live up to your expectations?" he asked. Once again, I found myself full of excitement, rattling off my impressions of the place. Toby sat and listened without interruption, as he could see the effect it had on me.

"Oh, I'm sorry, I lost myself. You were right, Toby, you have to experience it; words don't do it justice. Now it's your turn. What did you want to talk to me about?" Toby sat and looked at me, shaking his head.

"What's wrong?" I could see he was struggling with what he was about to say.

"What I'm about to tell you is going to come as a big shock to you, Beth. I have to warn you before I start. In fact, come and sit by me," he said as he patted the settee. My heart started to race, what could possibly be so wrong when I'm sitting next to him? I felt happy and privileged.

"We have found who took Alice, but we haven't been able to find her body …"

Before Toby could continue, my tears started. "Who would do this to a young girl? Who was it, Toby?" I cried. He reached for my hand before continuing; he needed to see if I could take it all in.

"The black hearse was the start, and from then on, all the evidence plus the DNA puts Phil at the crime scene." Toby told me Phil was denying all charges. After hours of searching the police had found some human hair in the hearse and the DNA confirmed it was from Alice! I let out a scream and felt Toby's arm enfolding me, "No, you have it all wrong. He's her father. Why would he want to hurt her? You've got it all wrong," I sobbed.

Toby was expecting a reaction, not this one though, but he was prepared. "I'm so sorry, Beth, that's why I haven't said anything, as we had to be sure. It all began when I first approached him about the hearse and he wanted to know why I was snooping around. That was when my suspicions began. When I went back and spoke to the owner, he told me Phil had asked to use the hearse that night. Then when I met him at your place he took off; he couldn't face me. I knew then it was him."

"But why Alice? Where is he now?" I asked. Toby said Phil was in custody at the police station. My head was spinning. My darling daughter had been murdered by her own father. How I hated him. When my head gradually cleared, I remembered my friend Alice then my daughter Alice; was it the name, had I sealed her fate by giving her that name, was I to blame? Here I was in Toby's arms sobbing. I leaned into him. I needed someone to hold me and tell me it was all a dream … but no, it was real.

Toby told me Phil was denying all charges. After hours of searching, the police had found some human hair in the hearse and the DNA confirmed it was from Alice. "We have no idea where her body is, and of course Phil is not going to help the police with any enquiries. He's denying everything, but we have enough evidence to know he was her abductor."

I was stunned. What had he done with Alice? I prayed to God she never suffered. I asked Toby if they had any idea what happened to her body. Toby hesitated before answering, "He must have taken her to the funeral parlour. We are still searching for evidence, but after that we don't know."

Toby moved away from me a little, so I sat up and apologised. "Don't be sorry, Beth. You needed to be comforted. You have been through more than a person should have to endure. I'm sorry It was me that had to bring you such shocking news. Are you okay?" I nodded, which was all I could manage. My mind was numb; where to from here? Suddenly I thought of James and Sarah; they would have to be told. My God, what were they going to think? Like me, they would be devastated.

"I'll leave you now, as you will need time to yourself. I'm here if you need me, so just call anytime." Toby hugged me and I thanked him and told him he was my rock. "Lean on me if you need to," were his parting words.

Bloody hell, what had Phil done? He had ruined my life completely! It was only then I noticed my half glass of wine. I hadn't even offered Toby a drink, but nothing seemed to matter any more. I picked up my wine and sipped away; would it help my problems disappear? Suddenly I thought of John. Why did he always come to my mind when I was facing a crisis? Not that he could help me, but he was a diversion. I decided to finish the bottle. If it numbed my brain, I would fall into bed and wake up to a new day.

My head felt like I had been hit with a hammer. Had I slept all night? How I wished I could have slept for another couple of days and let the world sort everything out... but no, I had a phone call to make. What would I say to the kids? Who would manage it best? Perhaps James. I called their number hoping James would answer and, yes, I got my wish. "Hi Mother, how are you? Is something wrong?" he asked. I choked. James was always straight to the point.

"James, the police have found Alice's abductor and have arrested him. He is in police custody."

"Oh, Mother, I'm so sorry. What happened to her?"

I told him her body had not been recovered so no one knew at this stage, but there was little hope of her being alive. He then asked if we knew the perpetrator. What was I going to say? I felt sick; how would he react? "I don't know how to break this to you, James, but you have to know. It is your father."

"Our father! It can't be. No, are you sure?"

"Yes, your father has been arrested. His DNA was

found on Alice's wheelchair, and he lied to the police," I said, as the sobbing started.

"Mother, Sarah and I will fly home on the first available flight. You need us. The bastard, why would he do that to Alice? I don't know how Sarah is going to take this. I will break it to her gently. You take care until we arrive. I'm so sorry, Mother." I could hear him crying as he said goodbye. God knows how Sarah was going to cope.

Thank goodness it was the weekend, and I didn't have to face anyone. Toby said no names would be released at that stage, so I was spared any agony for the moment. I walked around the house in a daze, still trying to work out why Phil had hurt Alice. I knew he didn't feel any connection to her, but why take her life? Things didn't add up, and I was totally confused.

I went into Alice's room and lay on her bed crying. My darling daughter was gone, but where was her body? I needed to know. My hatred for Phil intensified. I never wanted to see him ever again. How could I have loved someone so wicked? But did I ever really love him, or was it just a way to escape from my mother? I never had any of the feelings for Phil that I was experiencing with Toby.

It was only when I finally stopped crying that I heard the doorbell ringing. I couldn't answer it. I heard Toby calling me, "Beth, please answer the door. I know you are there". But I couldn't let him see me in this state, as my eyes were red and swollen, so I called to him. "I'm sorry, Toby, I want to be on my own. I'm okay, but just leave me alone today." With this the doorbell didn't ring again.

I had a look at my diary to see what appointments I

had for the start of the working week. There were only two for the Monday afternoon, and hopefully I could deal with them without breaking down. I knew Toby would be in touch, so I had to be prepared. All my romantic feelings had gone, as all I could do was think of Alice. What were her last thoughts? This was enough to start me off again. I slammed my hands on the table to let out my frustrations. It felt like I was falling apart, which brought on another bout of tears. All I could think of was my missing daughter; would her body ever be returned to us?

Monday was nearly over and I somehow managed to get through without a tear. I had to be strong for Alice's sake. As I was making my way home, I stopped off at the police station to let Toby know I was okay and thank him for being concerned. As I entered his office he stood up and came over and put his arm around my shoulders. "How are you today, Beth? What an ordeal you are going through. Have you told your children?" I told him they were on their way home, although I didn't know when they would arrive, as it depended on how soon they could get flights at such a short notice.

"Sit down, Beth, I want to talk to you. … We have tried to get Phil to tell us where Alice's body is, but he denies everything. We know from the evidence we have that he is guilty, but with all murder cases it's vital to find a body. I think he is going to be defiant, which makes it harder for us, as it could drag on. Do you think he might let something slip to James or Sarah?" I really didn't know so I told Toby what I thought. Sarah had detached herself from him, but James kept in touch. Toby suggested they speak with James when he arrived, to see if he could keep up a pretence in case Phil made a slip of the tongue, as they needed every bit of evidence against him.

Several days later, on arriving home there were James and Sarah waiting at the door. There were hugs all round amid tears. Sarah was the first to speak. "How could he do that, Mother? Our disabled sister and he murdered her. It makes me sick. I hate him, and I hope he rots in hell."

"Come on in, we can talk inside. I know you are angry; we are all angry he took Alice from us, but I keep asking myself why."

"Mother, he told James and me that you chose Alice over him, that she ruined your marriage." I was shocked to hear this. Is that what he really thought? He knew why our marriage soured, and it had nothing to do with our daughter.

"I'm so happy you are home, as I need you both." I noticed James was quiet so asked him why. "Mother, I am heartbroken. My father is a murderer. We have lost our Alice because of him. He had no feelings for her then he takes her life. I can never forgive him."

"I know, James, we all feel the same. Toby, the detective, wants to speak with you. He thinks our one hope of obtaining information that will incriminate Phil may be through your association with him. We have to bring Alice home so we can say our final goodbyes. We need you to remain on speaking terms with Phil. It will be hard, but it also may be of help.

A meeting was arranged with Toby. I wanted my family to meet him and see what they thought of him. Not that it really mattered, as nothing would change how I felt. They weren't to know my feelings, as not for one minute would they imagine their mother having feelings for someone so much younger.

We met at my office as I had cancelled my afternoon appointments. I introduced Toby to James and Sarah, then we all sat down to discuss Alice's disappearance. James asked Toby what he had on Phil, so he filled in all the details. "Alice's DNA was extracted from strands of hair found in the hearse. From there we are stumped as we don't know what he did with the body. He denies everything, but that's where you might be able to help us. Could you stay in contact with him? I know it won't be easy, but do you think it is possible?"

James looked at Toby. He felt he was a good guy to have on their side, as he had strategies in place. "I won't pretend it will be easy. I hate him for what he did, but if you think something may come from it, I will give it a go … no promises, though!" Sarah and James agreed that at whatever cost, we had to get Alice's body back with us, so we could give her the farewell she deserved.

Toby saw the heartache we were suffering as a family, so he worked long hours to find more evidence against Phil. He went back to the funeral parlour to see if there was anything he had missed on his earlier search. The embalming room had not been searched so this was where he would concentrate on. The owner was not happy, but since it was the police asking he had to agree to allow the search to go ahead. Toby found bits of fluff on the odd skirting board, so this was collected along with the inside bag of the vacuum cleaner, and a feather duster that was hanging on a hook. These items were taken to the forensic laboratory where DNA testing was carried out. It would take just one stand of hair from somewhere in this room to prove his theory, one which he hadn't discussed with anyone, but one he knew would involve people outside of this family.

A crucial piece of evidence

FOUR DAYS after presenting those items to the forensic laboratory, there was a breakthrough. On the feather duster was a strand of hair that was a match to Alice's DNA. Toby wasted no time in going back to find out about the feather duster. He spoke with the owner. "What is the duster used for and who uses it?" The owner told Toby it was used solely to dust the coffin before it left the funeral parlour. It was a special duster: the feathers were soft, so they didn't scratch the coffin. "Did Phil work in this room?" Toby asked. The owner told him that Phil never entered this room; it was only for the embalming people. Phil was the driver and looked after the hearses, so he definitely had no reason to be anywhere near this room. It was out of bounds to several of the staff. So then, why was Alice's hair on the duster? It pointed to one conclusion: Alice's body had been in this room. This cemented his theory, while hoping he would be proven wrong … but the evidence was there.

Toby went back to his office to ponder how he would handle this. He sat for several hours before making a decision. He went back to the funeral parlour to find out how many burials occurred around the dates of Alice's disappearance. He was shocked to find that it had been a particularly busy week with five burials. This was of great concern. Were the bodies going to be exhumed to see if one of the coffins contained two bodies instead of one? How was he going to break this to the family?

Meanwhile James had forced himself to visit his father. The moment he set eyes on him he wanted to turn around and walk back out. He hoped he could hide the hatred he felt towards him, but he would do anything if it would see him convicted as Alice's murderer. He hoped Phil might weaken and tell him where her body lay.

"Hi, son, thank you for coming to visit me. I haven't had any visitors; you are my first, apart from the bloody police, who never leave me alone. They think I had something to do with your sister's disappearance. You know I didn't. You were with me that night. Remember, it was my birthday."

"Yes, Father, I remember. You were angry with Mother for telling us about your past. We came home early as you weren't very good company. When you asked where Mother was, we told you she was waiting at home for Alice, as she had a late lecture at the university."

"I don't remember saying that. Mind you, that was

months ago now, and my memory is not as good as it used to be. How is your mother taking this?"

"You can well imagine; it is eating at her heart. She doted on Alice because of the lack of affection you gave her. You missed out on a lot by not accepting her. She was a gifted child and we all loved her. I can't imagine why this happened to her. Who would want to harm her? What do you think might have happened?"

"I don't know, son. Perhaps she was picked up after her lecture and driven somewhere else. It is hard to say really. Tell me all about your holiday." James was shocked at his lack of remorse. How had he ever liked this man?

I was surprised to receive a call from Toby wanting us to have a family meeting. The thought of him touching my shoulder as he always did, to my way of thinking, was acknowledgement that he might just have feelings for me, and perhaps this was wishful thinking, but it made me happy, so I held on to these thoughts. I did wonder what this meeting would be about. James was back at varsity finishing his honours degree and Sarah was still pondering her future. She was unsettled because Alice's case was going nowhere. Like me, she wanted closure. The case had come to a standstill, which affected us all.

We were seated at the dining-room table waiting on Toby to arrive for the arranged meeting. Within five minutes the doorbell rang and Toby greeted me with the usual shoulder touch, which brought a comforting warmth to me. Once at the table, he opened his briefcase and neatly arranged his papers.

"I have new evidence as to what might have happened

to Alice's body. This is going to be disturbing to hear, and it is only a theory, but I'm pretty sure my thoughts are on the right track. We have more DNA results resulting from hair found on a feather duster, which is only used to dust the coffins before they leave to be put in the hearse. This leads me to the possibility that Alice's body has been buried with someone else, in the same coffin."

I let out a scream, "No that couldn't happen. It's just not possible. Oh, how horrible!"

"Could that really happen?" asked James. Toby assured him it was probable, with the evidence pointing to that conclusion.

Sarah held my hand, as she could see I was in shock. I asked myself, "Could Alice already be buried?" I couldn't handle this thought as we had never had the chance to farewell her.

"Toby, what happens now?" asked Sarah.

"The worst scenario is we will have to exhume the five bodies that were laid the same week that Alice went missing. This is going to upset five families, who have laid to rest their loved ones. Now, this cannot go outside this room, as law enforcement would need to conduct a detailed investigation, to gather as much evidence as possible to support the need for multiple exhumations."

"What happens if the next of kin refuse to have their loved ones exhumed?" asked James.

"If the investigation needs are deemed compelling enough, a court order could override them, which seems unfair, but it has happened. I have a lot more investigating to do before we can even think of beginning these proceedings, as separate court orders would be needed for each family to exhume their loved ones.

"I am sorry to be the bearer of such devastating news, but we all want to find out what happened to Alice. It is good your children are home to look out for you, Beth. I'll keep in touch with updates. On this note, I will depart," he said as he stood up. I walked him to the door and held out my hand to shake his, then I noticed he held on a little longer than normal. "Oh Toby, if only you knew," I whispered to myself as the warmth flowed from him to me.

Both James and Sarah were impressed with Toby, but perhaps they wouldn't have been if they had known my feelings.

I carried on with my social work, but my heart was elsewhere. Where was my daughter's body? Was she lying in a grave with a total stranger? This thought horrified me and brought many tears. My past also kept flashing before my eyes. Where was John? I hadn't given up on him, and he always popped into my life at times of extreme stress; was he my guiding light? Then there was my friend Alice. All I wanted was to remember her and her plight, but now I was experiencing the heartache all over again with my own Alice.

Toby visited me at my office to tell me that there was enough evidence with the DNA findings to make a convincing case for exhumation of the bodies. The families would be contacted immediately, as the police had to keep up the pressure for the exhumation of the dead. The logistics of opening multiple graves simultaneously, in a short time frame, would be complex. But this cheered me up, to think there was action actually happening at last.

Toby was now consulting with legal experts, other law enforcement and forensic specialists, which was essential to navigate this complex situation. I could understand how upset the families would be, when told their loved ones had to be exhumed. Why did it have to come to this? If only Phil had owned up to his crime, then it would have ended here. He had not been told about the hair on the feather duster, so he had no idea the graves were going to dug up. The police had decided against Phil knowing this was going to take place. They wanted to prove that Alice's body had been put in a coffin with another body.

Several days later, Toby visited to tell us that three of the deceased families had agreed to have their family members exhumed, but two were against their graves being disturbed. When they were told a court order would be taken out, they wanted their solicitors to fight this. To make matters less complicated, it was agreed to exhume the first three which had consent, then worry about the other two when the time came. Hopefully, it didn't have to go any further.

Sarah and I were elated when Toby announced, "The excavators are starting tomorrow under the supervision of the cemetery management, to ensure it is conducted respectfully and within accordance with regulations. A forensic pathologist will be involved to oversee the exhumation process and conduct examinations once they get the coffins to the surface. Their expertise is crucial in examining and identifying the remains to determine whether the missing person is indeed present in the coffin. Hopefully we will have Alice's remains to bring back to you soon. I will be thinking of you. Good luck, Beth." The tears started, so Sarah and I held hands, anticipating good news.

I closed my office for a week while the exhumation was going on, as Sarah and I stayed inside and close to the phone. Toby promised to call us with up-to-date news. I was on edge and couldn't settle at anything, so I thought it only fair not to handle other people's worries when I had this huge one of my own. We weren't allowed near the cemetery as it was closed in the area where the machinery was working. The media were milling around trying to get a story, but the police were tight-lipped, as they didn't want anything published that would compromise the case. This had to be kept away from Phil, as a body was needed to close the case. All his denials would be in vain if the proof was before him, then hopefully a confession would be forthcoming.

My hatred of Phil was festering. How could I have even married him? But I told myself that I couldn't have foreseen what the future held. This brought on a flood of tears as I thought of my darling Alice. Would she have known it was her father who had abducted her? Oh my God, the very thought haunted me!

Toby called to let us know they had dug up two graves and the forensic pathologist had confirmed each one contained only one body; they were working on the third as he spoke. Perhaps this was the one that would surrender the evidence they were after. Sarah and I waited, hoping this was so, otherwise we would have to wait for a court order to be delivered to the two families who had denied access to their graves.

Several hours passed then the phone call. "Hi, Beth, the forensic pathologist has just confirmed there are two bodies in the third coffin. Because the burials were quite recent, there is hope that if any soft tissue remained, it would be used for DNA extraction. I can't tell you any more at the moment, but this is the break we desperately needed. I will call you later."

I burst into tears. We now knew where Alice's remains were, and that was all we could hope for at this late stage. Sarah cried with me. Now we could think of her funeral.

The next morning Toby brought the forensic pathologist to meet us and explain what was happening, as we were at a total loss. "I'm sorry you have to go through this, as I can't imagine how I would cope. I will explain where we go from here. First, we have to take great care to prevent contamination between the two sets of remains. For separate processing we take DNA samples from different parts of the remains and process separately to ensure there is no cross-contamination. Each individual has a unique combination of markers. I don't know if you have been told, your daughter was buried with an elderly male. Physical examination of the skeletal remains can provide clues about the identity of individuals such as age and sex, as well as anatomical features and injuries that have occurred."

I was upset to think Alice's body had lain in a coffin

with a total stranger, but I had to get over that and be thankful to have her coming back to us. The pathologist told us Alice's remains would be put into a coffin and sealed, as it was better to remember her as she was. Toby had instructed the pathologist to find out how Alice died and what injuries she may have suffered. It was going to take another week to finalise everything, so we had to have plenty of patience. Just to know what happened to her would bring final closure.

Guilty or not guilty

TOBY QUESTIONED Phil for the last time, to give him a chance to change his story on what had happened to Alice. He still denied he had anything to do with her disappearance. Now it was time to confront him and let him know they had a body. Toby watched as he told him they had exhumed a grave and found two bodies in a coffin. On hearing this, Phil came at him like a madman as now he knew he had been cornered. Toby tried to restrain him as he called for backup. Phil was then taken to a high-security holding cell.

A family meeting had been arranged by Toby, as he wanted to tell us what would happen to Phil. In all the panic and anticipation, my feelings for Toby had been laid aside and I wondered if they would return. I would find out when he visited. It was great having James and Sarah home to help me through this bleak dark period, but now I felt it was time for me again. I had let my meditation slip, as it was not the same as having my home to myself because my routine had been disrupted. Meditation could not be carried out with people buzzing around, as silence was the background one had to have.

The doorbell rang so I went and let Toby in. As he passed and touched my shoulder, the magic was back ... it hadn't gone after all! I could carry on living my love life in secret. I needed time to fantasise what I wanted to happen, but realistically it probably never would. Through meditation I had learnt to love myself. I came first, and after that whatever happened... Acceptance of life and what came with it made me able to cope. Meditation was shaping my life, enabling me to believe in myself so I desperately needed to return to it ... it was time for the kids to move out, and get on with their own lives.

Toby startled me by telling us he had talked with Phil. "He is going to plead not guilty, although the evidence we have points to him being the murderer. He is going to try to persuade the judge and jury he was the victim in all this. So be prepared! No way will he get away with it. He is only fooling himself; he is a desperate man who has wronged and who will pay for his crime. The trial is not for another three months, so try to get on with life. I'll keep in touch with any information that comes to hand."

"But you will come to Alice's funeral, won't you, Toby?" I asked. He told me to let him know when the arrangements were made. My heart sank, wondering when I would see him next. I hoped our meetings would go on forever. But hope was only that ... hope, nothing else. This didn't have to be the end of my dreams, however, as meditation had taught me to be accepting, to love myself, which was the first hurdle to get over, and I had achieved that, so my future would be up to me.

A week had passed, and I received a call from Toby. The pathologist had explained how he thought Alice had died, so Toby wished to see me. I told him to come after I had closed my office as it was better to hear the news away from work, but I wanted to meet soon to learn what had happened to Alice. I needed peace of mind.

"I understand, Beth. I will call around at seven o'clock tonight, if that is okay." Just to hear his voice was the tonic I needed. James had moved in with a girlfriend and Sarah was waiting until after the funeral, then she was off to a job in the centre of London. She wanted to move away from the East End to a more exciting life in the city.

When Toby arrived, he sat next to me on the settee. "This will be hard for you to hear, Beth, but you must know. Alice was hit on the head from behind, with a blunt instrument, and would have died instantly. She would not have suffered and probably didn't see it coming. She would not have seen her killer, which was a blessing. It was a vicious attack with deadly consequences."

On hearing this my emotions took over and I cried like a baby. Toby took my hand and assured me that Phil would pay dearly for his crime. He would get a life sentence and his life in jail would not be pleasant. An overwhelming sense of calmness overcame me. I could now get on and arrange Alice's funeral so we could say our final goodbye. Then memories from the past came back to haunt me. First, was my friend Alice, who would turn in her grave if she knew the boy who got her pregnant had murdered my daughter. Then there was John. I hoped his life was much happier than mine and that one day our paths would cross again … would it ever happen? What would a crystal ball reveal … and did I really want to know?

We wanted to keep the funeral low-key, otherwise every man and his dog would come as Alice's story had made the papers, so it was all out there. Pity would draw some people and nosiness, and for the want of a continuing story, the press would be there in full force. James suggested we invite those who had worked on the exhumation and of course Toby … we couldn't forget him!

There were no burial dates available for two weeks, as in the Greater London area there were multiple deaths each day, so this was putting a strain on the outlying areas. Although I begged for an earlier date, explaining Alice's circumstances, it was still impossible. This meant I had to continue my meditation in the privacy of my bedroom as Sarah was always up bright and early, thus breaking any silence that may have been available to me. She had to postpone her shift to the heart of London for another two weeks until after the funeral.

I was busy in my office again as I had cancelled all my appointments due to my commitment to Alice. Sarah was asked to select some prayers and readings for the funeral, then we could go through them together at night. I hadn't seen Toby during this time so was feeling a bit low. I needed a pick-me-up, so decided to call into the police station and personally invite him to Alice's funeral now that we had a set date.

As I entered Toby's office, he pulled up a chair for me, then squeezed my shoulder as I sat down. "How is everything going, Beth. Are you coping okay?" he asked as he stood beside me. I looked up and our eyes met. Suddenly, that warm feeling came back to me, which was all I needed to get back into my happy space. "I just called in to tell you we have a date for Alice's funeral. Please say you will come." Toby accepted my invitation and agreed to go to my home afterwards for afternoon tea.

Alice's funeral

THE DAY of the funeral was special, as it was time to say our goodbyes to Alice. So much had happened since her disappearance, it had been a lot to take in. The coroner had meticulously documented the condition of Alice's body and written a detailed report on the evidence collected during the exhumation process. This was the final report ensuring all legal requirements were met, as this was going to be needed in the future, at a court hearing.

The service for Alice was held in a little stone church and only invited guests were present. This didn't stop crowds of people gathering outside along with the media and their bulky cameras. The minister welcomed everyone then led the prayers we had chosen. Next, James spoke about Alice and her ability to overcome any obstacles or distractions that might hinder her. Because she was headstrong, nothing was insurmountable and he admired her tenacity, which was taken away far too soon. He spoke on behalf of Sarah, as they shared the same thoughts and love for their sister.

As James stepped down, Toby made his way to the microphone. I was not prepared for this; what was he going to say? He began, "I have nothing but admiration for this family, especially you, Beth. The sadness you have endured is insurmountable, and yet you carried on with your business of helping other people with their problems. This family has lost a valuable member in such tragic circumstances and have managed to stay close. I wish you all the best for the future. Please take care of each other." Toby's words brought tears to my eyes. I didn't know if it was due to his speech or because of the place he held in my heart.

At last, my darling daughter was at peace, and I could visit her whenever I wished. We all made our way back to my home where afternoon tea and beverages were waiting to be served. Sarah popped the top off a couple of bottles of wine and filled some glasses and asked people to help themselves. As I reached for a glass, another hand reached for the same one, so two hands came together. Without looking, I knew who it was, and a hot tingle ran down my spine. A couple of seconds passed before I withdrew my hand, picked up another glass and apologised profusely. Then I asked myself, why did Toby not withdraw his hand? Was this intentional?

"Thank you, Toby, your speech was unexpected so

thank you for your kind words, and, yes, we are a close family. You have played a huge part in this investigation. If not for you, we might not have been standing there today, farewelling Alice. Again, thank you for your dedication to bringing Alice's murderer to justice. This means so much to me." Toby looked at me and said it had been his pleasure to have met us all. "Do call into the station if you need to talk. When Phil's trial starts, we will be in touch again. Take care of yourself, Beth." With these words he hugged me.

I held on to him; I didn't want to let him go, then suddenly I found myself expressing to him how I felt. Did I really say that? How stupid, I scolded myself. "I know your feelings, Beth, so don't be embarrassed. Everyone is entitled to feel as they wish." Why did he have to be so damn accommodating in every situation? Just then James came over to speak to Toby. This left an awkward moment unanswered, but that was okay. I thought I had been discreet with my feelings, but was I kidding myself?

The day after Alice's funeral, James, Sarah and I visited the cemetery and laid some fresh flowers. This would be our last visit as a family for quite some time, as the kids were taking off to London for work. They promised to come back when Alice's headstone had been installed. We linked hands and silently said our own prayers to our beloved Alice. She would never be forgotten, and our love for her would live on. My prayers included those to my best friend Alice and to John, who were both forever in my mind. It looked as if my life was leaning towards living on memories. Even the man who had touched my heart was never going to be anything but a dream, or perhaps a memory. Was I destined to live in the past?

Now that I had my home to myself again, I could focus on my meditation without interruptions. My meditation was the first thing I did after a shower, before breakfast. I believed in the saying 'empty stomach, empty mind'. This put me in a good place to begin my day. My focus didn't stray but was fixed on whatever came along.

I had a particularly busy day ahead as my appointment book was full, due to my time off. My first client was a desperate mother wanting advice on her daughter, aged fourteen, who was being pressured into having sex with her boyfriend. She didn't want to lose the boyfriend, so asked her mother if she could go on the pill. This was of course where the problem lay, as the family's religious beliefs did not allow it. The mother had tried to reason with her daughter, but at the age of fourteen reason did not come into it. She wanted to please her boyfriend, so they were at loggerheads.

"What can I do? I don't want to fall out with my daughter, but I can't go against my religious beliefs." I thought hard on this for several minutes. At the age of fourteen she was too young to be pressured to have sex, so perhaps he was the one that needed talking to. If he was threatening her to please himself, he wasn't a nice type of guy.

"Would you be upset if I talked to your daughter? I asked.

"Would you? Then that would save me from falling out with her."

We made an appointment for her to come and see me after my last appointment of the day.

The day flew by and at 5.30 a young girl came into my office. "Hi, I'm Leila, my mother said you wanted to talk to me." I asked her to sit down while I closed the door. "Tell me, Leila, how old are you?" I asked, while already knowing her age. "How old is your boyfriend?" was my next question. "He is twenty-one and is doing a carpentry apprenticeship. I really like him," she said. He was too old for her, so now I had some ammunition. "Do you realise that if he has sex with you, he is committing a crime, as you are underage? Do you want him to have a criminal conviction against his name? He could even go to prison for having sex with a minor; you wouldn't like that to happen.

"I was young once and this happened to me. My boyfriend pressured me, but I was strong and said no. It was the best thing, as several years later I met someone else, and was happy I said no, then I had no regrets. You are still very young, Leila, so don't rush and make decisions that you may later regret. Go out with your friends and have fun. If your boyfriend was a sensible guy, he would know it wasn't right for him to pressure you. Let him meet someone his own age. You are still a child, and he is an adult, and as an adult his way of thinking is not your way.

"Your mother is worried about you, and she wants to be your friend, but she is afraid for you. She loves you,

Leila, and that is a huge plus, as so many parents don't care. Please remember there are consequences with having sex, and in the end, it is the girl's life that is ruined. Men move on. Be a fourteen-year-old and have fun with your friends."

Leila looked at me, then got out of her chair, gave me a hug and thanked me. Had I done enough to convince her that he was too old for her? Several days later, Leila's mother called into my office to let me know Leila had broken up with her boyfriend. Leila was sad, but she had said no to his advances, and he dropped her. "Whatever you said to her did the trick, so thank you. If I had to deal with her, it might have ended differently."

The kids had come back for the unveiling of Alice's headstone. It was a sad time but now the worst was behind us. To me it was final, as now I could go to the cemetery and lay the flowers on something tangible. I could read the headstone with our message to Alice and feel at peace.

Several months later, I received a phone call from Toby. No, he had not slipped my mind; he was well and truly ingrained there, but I still had to function. I was good at giving advice but not so good at receiving it. He called to say a date had been set for Phil's trial, so he wanted to make me aware of this. "How has life been, Beth?" he asked. I told him I was fine, although my heart told me otherwise. Work was keeping me busy, and I was enjoying my own space. "We are bringing Phil back to our cell block for his trial. He is insisting he didn't do it and will plead not guilty. The jury will undoubtedly think otherwise, as the evidence we have against him puts him there at the scene."

"Well, I never want to see him again," I let Toby know. He reminded me I would have to attend the trial, as I may or may not be called upon to give evidence. This I was not looking forward to.

The trial

On the day before the trial, Toby came to my office to see how I was coping. I told him I felt numb. He asked if James and Sarah were coming to be with me. "They wanted to come but it meant taking time off work, so I told them not to worry as I thought I could manage. If it becomes too tough, James will come home and support me." Toby told me he would be there each day, so I could rely on him for support. This was an offer I certainly would not refuse, and it would be the only good thing about the hearing. Would this be a chance for me to express my feelings once again or was I aiming too high? First, I had to get through the night before the trial, thinking of all that had happened and being anxious about what lay ahead.

As I entered the courtroom in the morning, I felt sick at the thought of seeing Phil. How would I react, could I hold myself together? The room was full of people, some I knew but most were strangers. I wondered why there would be so many people present, but it was an unusually sad case of a father accused of murdering his disabled daughter. People were sympathetic and wanted to see justice take its course.

I sat down, my heart racing, then a friendly hand touched my shoulder, and I knew instantly who it was. "How are you holding up, Beth? I'm not able to sit with you, but I won't be far away. I will meet you in the foyer when the case is adjourned for the day. Stay strong. I will be thinking of you," then there was silence. Toby was gone. As I looked up people were staring at me, some even pointing, so I knew I had been recognised.

I watched as the jury were selected and sworn in, then they took their seats in the jury box. The defendant was brought in handcuffed to a police officer, then he was released to sit at the defence table alongside his attorney. I was shocked as I glanced at Phil. I hardly recognised him; he had aged and looked nothing like the man I once knew. The courtroom was abuzz with comments as he sat down, in fact a call of 'murderer' could be heard coming from the floor. The clerk of the court asked for silence, as the judge was about to enter. "All rise," he announced, signalling everyone in the courtroom to stand.

The judge appeared and when he was seated the clerk announced that the court was now in session. The judge gave a brief outline of the case at hand, then provided preliminary instructions to the jury before the trial began. I looked around to see if I could see Toby, and there he was sitting close to the prosecutor's table. He had explained he was not allowed to sit with me or any family members, as he had to maintain the appearance of impartiality. I couldn't bring myself to look in Phil's direction again, so I didn't know if he was looking at me. He meant nothing to me now.

"I will call upon Mr Toby Metcalf as a witness to establish the facts of the case," announced the judge. Toby walked to the witness stand and set his papers down. He addressed the judge, then carried on with the evidence he had. I listened carefully to what he was saying, wondering how Phil was reacting, so I sneaked a peek, only to see a total stranger showing no emotion, just a blank stare. Our eyes met and I froze. I quickly looked away, feeling a fool.

The day went by fast as the witnesses were called. There were direct examinations and cross examinations. I tried to take it all in but being in the same room as Phil filled me with hurt and hatred. I wanted it all to end. As the day drew to a close, the judge formally adjourned the court and announced it would reconvene at 10am the next day. I watched as the jurors left the jury box, wondering what was going on in their minds. Surely this was a cut-and-dried case, and Phil was a murderer … there was no doubt!

Toby was waiting for me in the foyer. I tried to hide my tears, but they insisted on coming. "I'm sorry, Toby, just the sight of that man makes me want to shout 'murderer'. I can't believe he was once part of my life, but he is like a stone statue now."

"Tomorrow is going to be hard for you, when Phil takes the stand. You will probably hear things that will upset you, but be brave as he will hang himself. The jury will see through him. Close your eyes and pretend you're somewhere else, somewhere pleasant."

Yes, I could imagine the two of us on a tropical island somewhere in the Pacific ... just the two of us! All the same I don't think Toby would imagine he was part of my 'somewhere else'.

Back at the court for the second day, the first person called to take the stand was Phil. He took the oath and swore on the Bible to tell the truth. He was asked to tell the court his account of the accusations against him. He started off with the fact that his daughter Alice had always come before him, and he felt rejected. He rambled on about the unfair treatment he received from his wife and how his daughter was never close to him.

"But you never acknowledged your daughter from the day she was born. You chose to disregard her because of her disabilities, is that not so?" asked the prosecutor. Phil hung his head and shrugged this question off. "All the evidence points to you being the only person who could have done this to Alice. Who else would want to murder an innocent young girl? She didn't have any enemies. Her DNA was found in the hearse from your work. You had borrowed the vehicle that day. And the special duster, which was only used to give the coffins their final dust before they left the funeral parlour, also contained Alice's DNA. That was the final clue as to where we could start looking for her body. How do you explain these findings?"

Phil talked on about his life, how he had worked for the same employer all these years and was a trusted employee. When their daughter Alice was born, their marriage turned sour, as all his wife's attention was bestowed on her. She didn't fulfil her marital duties, which left him feeling hurt. Then he turned to the night of the alleged crime. "I was with my other children James and Sarah that night. We were celebrating my birthday, so I couldn't have done it," replied Phil.

"But James and Sarah left early because you weren't in a good mood. You knew Alice was at night class, which was why your wife didn't come to dinner with you. Were you angry because Beth wasn't there?"

"Once again Alice was put before me, so yes I was angry, but I didn't murder Alice."

"That will be all," said the prosecutor.

It would be left to the jury to decide if Phil, in his anger, took revenge. Another day had come to a close, and the judge announced the court would reconvene at 10.30am. I felt exhausted so sat on the bench seat in the foyer. Within minutes Toby arrived and took my hand. "That went well today, Beth. Phil painted a pretty untidy picture of himself to the jurors, putting all the blame on you for making Alice a priority over him. He was wallowing in his own self-pity, and there was no love shown towards Alice . She deserved your attention, for God's sake. He is an adult and should have understood this. The case is going against him. I think tomorrow we will see the jury convene."

"I hope so Toby, I'm about done. It all happened months ago and I'm over it. Thanks to you I now have a place to visit, and I can talk to Alice and let her know how

I'm feeling. It's what keeps me sane at times when I'm down."

Toby squeezed my hand. "It will soon be over, then you can get on with your life, meet new friends, and have fun. That's what lies ahead Beth. When this case is over, we will go for a drink and celebrate."

Why was he so damn young? He said all the right things at the appropriate times, and he was caring and knew how to treat a woman.

It was now day three, and there was a lot of cross-examining taking place. Early in the afternoon the judge asked both sides to present their closing arguments, summarising their cases and trying to persuade the jury to their point of view. The judge then provided the jury with legal instructions how they should deliberate. The jury left the courtroom to retire to the jury room to reach a verdict. The judge told the court the case would reconvene the next day at 11.30am, thus hoping the jury would return with their verdict.

Toby couldn't stay to talk with me as he had another appointment. I stopped off at my office, which was closed for the week while the trial was on. There were several calls on my answer machine, so I attended to them then headed home. I later made my nightly calls to James and Sarah.

I spent most of the night awake, hoping the jury would return a guilty verdict. Then I wouldn't have to think of Phil for many years. He would be locked away and I hoped he would have time to reflect on the pain he had inflicted on others. Alice meant nothing to him, but she meant the world to me. If he had accepted her, things at home would have been completely different.

I made my way to court and was greeted by Toby in the lobby. "Morning, Beth. I hope the jury has come to a verdict, then we can go for that drink later. I want it to be over today so you can have closure." I nodded in agreement. Suddenly a young woman came up to me and said she prayed the jury would find the defendant guilty. I was taken by surprise, but when I looked at her, her face seemed familiar, then the penny dropped. She was the junior who was hired after me at the funeral parlour, the one that Phil dated after I refused his advances. But why would she say that?

"You probably don't know, but Phil got me pregnant and when I told him, he dropped me and went back to you. He is nothing short of a coward," she spat out. My heart stopped for a moment, then I thought back to the day when Phil met me at the gate of the child-care centre. Did he come back to me simply because of the predicament he was in? That was all I needed … to think of myself as a rebound! This totally shocked me. I ran to the cloakroom and the tears followed. After a couple of minutes, I realised I should be in the courtroom, so quickly bathed my eyes to help reduce the redness.

The courtroom was packed as everyone was hoping for a verdict today. A kind person moved over so I could be seated. Everyone stood up as the judge entered. He made his way to the bench then asked everyone to be seated. "Have you finished your deliberation and reached a verdict?" he asked the jurors.

"Yes, your honour, we have reached a verdict."

"How do you find the defendant, guilty or not guilty?"

"We find the defendant guilty of first-degree murder."

A hushed silence came over the court, then it was broken as I screamed out "Murderer!" Phil turned and looked at me, but all I could see were eyes as cold as stone. I had to get out of the courtroom. I felt I was suffocating and I needed some fresh air. Then I partially collapsed onto a seat outside the court. This was where Toby found me. My face was tear stained as I recalled the conversation with the other woman.

"What's wrong, Beth? You should be happy," he said. I burst into tears again as I told him what the young woman had said to me.

"The bastard. Thank God he is going away for a long time. He won't be able to hurt you any more. Try and forget him Beth; that is all history. Focus on the future. Do you feel like that drink today?" I wasn't in the right frame of mind, so asked Toby if we could leave it until the next day. I needed time to absorb what I had learnt ... a rebound ... that was hard to take, and it totally deflated me. What a mess I had made of my life. My thoughts drifted back to John, which always happened in a crisis. Was he happy? His life must be better than mine!

I didn't take much rocking to get to sleep. I was totally exhausted and my body felt like butter. I flopped on to the bed and pulled up the bedclothes, after which I remember nothing. My lights had gone out completely! When I woke, I got the shock of my life ... it was 10.30am. Was this telling me to slow down, to take more care of myself ... but would I listen?

I had missed a phone call and there was a message: "Toby here, Beth. I will pick you up at five o'clock. If I don't hear from you, I will assume it is okay." If not for the age difference I would gladly seduce Toby. I was sure we both had sexual feelings that we might like to exchange! The rest of the day slipped by; I couldn't settle at anything while still thinking about being used by Phil. I didn't ask the girl who replaced me as a junior at the funeral chapel if she had kept Phil's child. Perhaps James and Sarah had a half-brother or sister.

The next big question was what I would wear to go for drinks with Toby. I didn't want him to think I was past my use-by-date, but then again if I dressed too young, I was only kidding myself. I settled for sensible dress: a white frilly blouse and black trousers. After all, it was just for drinks. On the dot of five o'clock the doorbell rang. I was surprised as I had only ever seen Toby in a suit, and here he was in casual clothing, but he looked every bit as inviting in his casual style.

"Right, Beth, away we go. I'm taking you to a little pub where I used to hang out many years ago. You might even be lucky enough to see a photo of me."

"That sounds exciting." We left the East End and headed out until we hit the motorway, on which we drove for thirty minutes until we turned off to a side road and pulled up outside a quaint old pub. Toby opened the car door for me and we walked inside, where he led me to a table at the back of the bar. The wall was covered in sporting photos.

"I bet you can't pick me in this photo?" he asked. I stood and looked, but they were young boys. I couldn't see a resemblance to any of the boys. But when he pointed it out to me, yes, I could see a likeness. "My team won several cups and trophies playing on the football grounds here, that's why I love coming back."

"So, you just wanted to show off a little. Is that why you brought me here?" I teased. He explained it was nice to leave the area where he worked and where he couldn't relax. He asked if he could get me a wine, to which I nodded. Instead of a glass he brought back a bottle. "Here's to a new future, Beth. You deserve it for all you have been through. I'm only sad I didn't meet Alice in person, but I feel I did know her in spirit." We touched glasses and sipped our wines. We talked freely about everything and the time passed so quickly, while the wine flowed … soon the bottle was empty.

"We may as well have a bite to eat while we are here. Is that okay with you?" he asked. I agreed. I loved every moment with him, even his company was enough if that was all I was entitled to; dreams could come later. He asked if I wanted another wine, but I declined as I didn't want my feelings to be exposed and ruin these special moments.

After we had eaten, Toby offered to pay but I insisted that I pay my share. That was not to be, as he went to the counter and did the deed. "Toby, I don't expect you to pay for my dinner," I protested. "But I wanted to Beth. I've enjoyed your company." We drove back to the East End and pulled up at my home. I tried to put money in Toby's jacket pocket, our hands touched, and neither of us withdrew. I felt his hand hold mine and I couldn't help myself; I leaned over and kissed his cheek. Embarrassment set in; what had I just done? I apologised and quickly opened the car door and ran inside.

That was the last I saw of Toby for several months, but he didn't leave my mind, and I was back living on memories and my past once again. My workload had doubled, as now I was known to many people due the high-profile murder case. People were most sympathetic towards me; this is what attracted them to my workplace. I was able to help them make choices and offer them advice, but the end decision was theirs to make. Because I was getting more cases than I could handle, I took on a junior clerk and a qualified case worker. This worked out well as I didn't have to spend time on the phone booking people in for appointments. That was now all done for me.

One day while at the office, I was surprised by a visit from Toby. "Hi Beth, you look as if you are really busy. Is everything okay with you?" he asked. I told him my business was keeping me out of trouble, then I enquired as to how he was. "I've just come to tell you I have been offered a promotion out of town, in fact in Edinburgh, so I just wanted to ask you out for a farewell drink." My heart missed a beat. He was leaving me, and I would never see him again. I wanted to burst out in tears. "When are you leaving, Toby?" I asked. He told me he only had two weeks left until he started his new job. I had to remind myself this love affair was between me and the brick wall, and no one else knew, not even Toby! "Will Friday at five o'clock be fine? I'll pick you up from your place." I nodded in agreement; Friday night it was.

Now I was faced with the same dilemma, what to wear out for a drink. This time I would be a little bolder. I was never going to see him again so I decided to make a statement, one I hoped he would remember. I went shopping; this was a special occasion, so I needed a special dress. I loved colour, so colour it was. I even bought shoes to match. It was fun as I hadn't been clothes shopping for a long while.

I waited patiently for Toby to arrive. This time he was a little late which was unusual for him, perhaps he had decided not to come. My lip went down when suddenly I heard his car pull up. I waited until he came to the door, as I didn't want to seem too keen, but if the truth be known I would have waited on the street for him.

"My, you look lovely tonight, Beth. I love your dress. Colour suits you."

"I bought it specially for this outing," I let him know in a cheeky manner. He opened the car door for me – such a gentleman. He drove downtown to a little pub which I had not been to before. We found a quiet table and sat down. "What do you fancy drinking tonight, Beth?" I decided not to be boring so asked for the house cocktail of the night. He came back with two; hopefully he felt like a bit of fun tonight! He told me about the new job he had been offered, which was in fact solving a murder case similar to Alice's, and he hoped for the same conclusion. It was a cold case, but new evidence had turned up so now it was his to solve. "I like a challenge, something I can get my teeth into, instead of unimportant jobs," he said. I couldn't help but give him praise. "You will do well, Toby, you're a great guy and I know you won't let anything beat you. I've seen that look in your eyes."

He picked up the glasses and took them to get refilled. As he was walking back someone tapped him on the shoulder and asked what he was doing here. Toby told him he was with a very good friend. "This is Beth," he said as he introduced us. "Can I join you?" he asked. Toby looked at me and I nodded. Just my luck, I thought to myself, now I have to share him. The guys talked away as the friend was also in the police force.

"So, you are leaving I hear, I'll miss you, mate. I followed that case you just solved. Fancy that bugger murdering his own daughter, what a low life. The poor wife she must have been devastated, fancy living with a murderer and not knowing. I'm glad you nailed him." Toby looked at me; he certainly hadn't seen that coming.

"Yes, it was a sad case, but the wife is a survivor, in fact she is a very nice lady," Toby said as he winked at me. That will do, I told myself.

"Well, I had better let you guys have a bit of time together," the friend said as he got up to leave. Toby apologised as soon as the guy left.

"It's not your fault; he wouldn't have expected you to be out with a murderer's wife," I joked. Toby scolded me, "Don't ever think of yourself as that Beth. You are a successful business woman. You have the world at your fingertips." I thought for a moment then decided to go for it. "No, I haven't really Toby, the person I want I can't have, that's the sad truth."

"What do you mean, Beth? Surely you are not referring to me?" he asked. What could I say? It was now or never. "Yes, Toby it's you I want. You are a lovely guy, but our ages are against us."

"I'm flattered, Beth. I thought you liked me as a friend. If I was a few years older, yes, there could have been something, but unfortunately, I'm a married man."

"I know that Toby, but let's enjoy tonight. We will have one more drink." This time I took the glasses up to be refilled. I felt good, now that he knew how I felt. The situation was never going to change. Toby asked me about my business, so I told him the trial had brought in new clients, and I had two new staff. "You will do well, Beth, and one day you will meet someone who will make you very happy. You are a lovely lady and deserve happiness."

As we were driving home Toby told me he felt privileged to have met me, and he reached across and took my hand. When we pulled up at my home he leaned across and kissed my cheek. I reciprocated and before long we were exchanging passionate kisses. This time I didn't apologise as we both knew there was something there, which we couldn't have. I opened the car door and thanked Toby and wished him all the best for his future. I never looked back as my eyes were full of tears. It was like the end of a love affair, it hurt so much.

As the next few years went by, I immersed myself in

work. I could never let go of the image of Toby or my feelings for him. I was back living on memories and my past. I thought more about John now, wondering what sort of life he was living. In the meantime, I would live my life in the East End of London and hope one day happiness would find me! I had made a big decision not to go back to my old self and become a slouch with my appearance. Meditation had taught me to love myself first, to be happy with who I was and take pride in myself. If an opportunity presented itself for me to fall in love again, I would be ready. Until that happened, I had myself to love, and that was all I needed at this time. I had a career that was fulfilling, because I could help other people. My life was okay!

The retreat

I FELT I needed time away, so decided to attend a health and meditation retreat to forget Toby and try to move on. My staff would carry on and take care of business while I was away. I needed to do something fulfilling for myself. The retreat was in the countryside away from the hustle and bustle of city life, where the outside world could be forgotten. This is just what I needed: for my past few years to be wiped from my mind, even if it was only for the two weeks there. We were allowed to bring a photo of someone dear to us, who we could sit on our dresser to make our room feel more like home. Of course I took a photo of my daughter Alice.

When we arrived, we were given our own room for the fortnight. We all met for drinks in the lounge and were given name badges which we had to wear all the time. The drinks were fruit juices, and the snacks were sticks of carrot and celery accompanied by dips. We were introduced to the staff who would be interacting with us, and they were a mix of men and women. The owner of the retreat introduced herself as Sophia and promised us all a rewarding stay.

At six o'clock a chime signalled that dinner was ready, so we made our way to the dining room. The decor was welcoming with colours of red and gold and several Buddha statues were placed around the room. We were asked to find our names at the table, and that was where we sat each mealtime. I was in the middle of the long table so had a person each side. We introduced ourselves to our immediate neighbours and started chatting. When the food arrived, it looked amazing –healthy salads and cheeses, along with chicken and a large array of fresh fruits, and grain breads. You certainly knew you were at a health resort!

A staff member came in after we had finished dinner and asked us to assemble in the lounge. He told us, "This is a place of peace and friendship, so each night after we have finished our dinner we will assemble here. Tonight, we will introduce ourselves and tell our age … this is one of the deepest secrets we hold dear, but now we are going to share this secret with everyone, although we are total strangers tonight, tomorrow we will all be friends."

We were all a little bit nervous, but our teacher started off with his introduction and age, and after the first couple of people spoke, we all knew we had to have a turn. This was to break down any barriers we had and put us all on a level footing.

At ten o'clock we were asked to go to our rooms and in

the morning turn up for breakfast in the dining room at seven o'clock. We were not allowed to bring laptops, computers or cell phones with us, as we were experiencing time out with nature, with no distractions.

As I climbed into my bed the aroma of lavender came from my pillow; it was a soothing herb that was meant to help with sleep. I snuggled into my pillow and my thoughts went to John, wondering if he was married and had children, and what sort of job he worked at. Did he join up to fight in the war after he left us? I don't know why he came to me tonight; were we meant to focus on someone from the past? I must have dropped off to sleep after these thoughts, only to be woken by a chime. I jumped out of bed to find it was 6am. I must have slept soundly. I sat on my bed and did a quick meditation, then jumped in the shower, got dressed ready to be at breakfast at 7am.

In this intake there were twelve people, eight women and four men, which surprised me, as I thought this would only be of interest to women. As I came out of my room the man from next-door came out at the same time, so we walked together to the dining room. We sat down at our given places at the table and were introduced to our teacher who would be taking us for meditation. Our breakfast consisted of cereal, fruit, porridge and brown bread for toast. Everyone seemed to be happy, and we were all looking forward to our next session.

We were led into a large room where there were thirteen mats on the floor. We were asked to pick a mat and sit on it and put our palms flat on our knees. "This morning we are going to learn to meditate. Before I start, does anyone here meditate?" he asked. I put up my hand expecting others to follow but I was the only one. I felt embarrassed as all eyes looked my way. "Nice one, Beth. Please stand up and tell us what you get from meditating." I began, "First, I had to learn to love myself, to believe in myself, and not let anyone take from me what is mine and that was self-respect."

"Very good, Beth, thank you, you have nailed it. Would I be right in saying you have been deeply hurt and that is why you turned to meditation?" I nodded. "Right class, we start with our eyes closed and taking deep breaths. Breathe deep into your chest, hold, then exhale out all that stale air. This will clear your mind and while you concentrate on your breathing, all else will be blocked out, no thoughts will get through so your mind will not wander, it will be at peace, and you will feel the silence. You will sit here for one hour doing this. Then we will walk among the trees and take in the beauty of nature that surrounds us. This will end our session, thank you all."

Lunch came next. It was a smorgasbord of healthy foods. Then we were given an hour to relax and following this was a massage session. I was looking forward to being pampered as I had never experienced this before. I went back to my room and picked up my photo of Alice and clutched it to my chest. This was the pain my teacher was referring to. It is a shame that you have to wait for a crisis to happen to begin a healing journey, when it was available all the time. No other class members had meditated, so now they were at a distinct advantage when they had to face a crisis; they would be prepared.

Now I was on my way to the much-awaited massage. I was given two large white towels to wrap around me, one for the top half and the other for the bottom half, then had to lie on the table face down. My masseuse introduced herself, then explained she would take the top towel off and lay some hot stones on my back. This was deep-heat therapy. When they cooled, she would remove them and use her hands to massage from my waist to my neck and then on to my shoulders. Her hands were powerful as she pushed hard on pressure points, I certainly knew she was there. This felt good, and as she hit the pressure points the pain was more intense. "You will feel pain, but it is good pain as it is loosening up your tense muscles. Be brave because after this session you will feel sore, but that will disappear when you get into the therapeutic pool and relax."

She then replaced the towel over the top half of my body and folded the lower towel so she could work on my legs. The hot stones were placed along my leg muscles, then when they cooled she worked her hands. My body hurt but she had warned me this is what I would feel. My leg muscles were tight, and by massaging them, it would free them up. I couldn't wait to get into the hot pool.

While in the pool, a younger woman made herself known to me. I did think for a moment I knew her, but where I asked myself, was she a past client? I had noticed her at our meditation class, as she had smiled at me, and I had smiled back. It was only when she mentioned her name that I realised this was the person who spoke to me at Phil's trial, the girl that had taken the junior position at the funeral parlour just before I left. I was stunned. I didn't know what to say. In my mind there was so much I wanted to ask her, but when confronted with the situation, I was dumbfounded.

"Please don't be angry with me. I thought you recognised me," she said. When I finally found my tongue, I asked if we could hold this discussion at another time, as my body had now tensed up and I felt the massage was a waste of time. This was the effect Phil had on me. With that, she moved away and started talking with someone else. I closed my eyes. This was a continuation of Phil always popping up in my life. Why couldn't he be forgotten forever? As I was leaving the pool I saw her watching me, so I went over and asked if she would like to come to my room to talk. It was no good letting it fester, as there were things I had to know. We had two hours before the dinner chime.

It wasn't long before there was a knock on my door. I called for her to come in and sit down. She was wearing her name tag with the name Julie on it. I couldn't remember her name from the funeral parlour days. "What would you like to know?" she asked.

"You mentioned at the trial that Phil had got you pregnant. Did you keep the baby?"

"Yes, it was a little girl, and she was born with a defect. She is in a wheelchair," she replied. I couldn't believe what I had just heard.

"Did Phil know there was something wrong with her?"

"He walked out on me when I told him I was pregnant, then he told me he was going to get back with you. He used to visit me when he was with you. He never held the baby; he didn't like the fact that something was wrong with her."

I burst into tears. Not only had he ruined my life, he had ruined someone else's. Julie continued, "He offered to pay me for sex as he knew I was struggling. I needed money, so I gave into him and gave him sex. He wouldn't give me money for our baby; he said I had to earn it. I'm sorry you had to hear this, but when I couldn't stand him any more and stopped having sex with him, he never came back. I hated him and myself for what I let him do to me, but I needed the money for our little girl."

"Did Phil tell you about our little girl having a disability? She was in a wheelchair too."

"No, he never told me. It was only when he went up for murder and I read it in the newspaper that I found out. My mother looks after my daughter. Her name is Alice..."

"Just a minute," I interrupted. "Who named her Alice?"

Julie said Phil wanted to name her Alice, and as she hadn't thought of a name that's what she called her. "What the hell, he was sick in the head," I told myself. Why would he want to call her Alice? Was it after my best friend Alice, because at this stage our daughter wasn't even born. This was turning into a bigger nightmare than I could have imagined. Perhaps he did love my friend and when she disappeared, he missed her. Did he want to keep her memory alive? It was all becoming too much.

To think he was still having sex with Julie while

married to me, but to be paying for it and not giving her money to support the baby. He was definitely not right in the head! Then I remembered the nights he didn't come home. Was this where he was, paying Julie to have sex with him?

"How did you manage when the money stopped from Phil?"

"My mother looked after Alice and I went to work. I met an older man, and he liked me so I married him. We had a son together. He has been good to Alice and me, that's why I am here today, because he wanted to treat me to something special."

"Oh Julie, I'm so happy that it has all worked out for you. To think Phil was a blight on us both, but not any more thank God, and he is paying for all his actions now. It will never bring my Alice back, but I have lovely memories of her. I visit her grave every week and take her flowers and talk to her. This is a photo of her. I take it wherever I go."

"Gosh, she looks a little like my Alice; there is a likeness there," said Julie. All of a sudden, we were disturbed by the dinner chime.

After dinner we had our nightly meeting where we all had to tell a little about our lives. This was called the sharing session so that we could all get to know something about each other. Tonight, the subject was work, so we had to talk about our careers. Each night was a different subject, but we didn't know what the subject was until we entered the room and saw it on the whiteboard. We were then given five minutes to think about what we were going to say. There were no paper or pens; it had to come straight from the brain. It certainly made us conscious of how quick our brains worked.

A fortnight had passed, and this was our last day at the retreat. It was a free day to do whatever we liked, as many had made friends so were spending their last day together. I had enjoyed every session and took away something from each one. My mind was more open to things I didn't think mattered, but I learned everything mattered, it was just how you handled it that determined the result. Positivity was the key word! I learned most things that were negative could be made positive with the right mindset. What I had learnt at this retreat would certainly help me in my job, and it was of huge benefit to me, especially when dealing with other people's problems.

After lunch my meditation teacher called me aside as he wanted to speak with me one on one. He wanted to know what dark experience I had faced in life that had made me turn to meditation. I told him about Alice, Phil and the murder trial. That I was at rock bottom and had to search for something to help get me through, as my self-esteem was at my lowest. I went to a four-day meditation class, which helped me immensely, so I carried on and now it had become an everyday occurrence. Once I learned to love myself, and was able to say, "I accept who I am", there was a light that showed the way for me to see there was still life ahead. It had helped me survive a traumatic time in my life.

He asked me if I would consider coming to the retreat and speaking to people who were trying to overcome trauma. They held different courses from time to time and what I had been through, and come out the other side, was, he said, amazing. It showed people could be faced with the worst possible difficulties and still survive to become positive human beings again.

"If it is not too traumatic for you to tell your story to others, you'll be able to let them see an example of a resilient person who defied all odds, found her self-esteem, and carried on being there for others. I think you'd be a wonderful advocate as a teacher here at the retreat. Please think about it and let me know as soon as you have made up your mind, Beth."

I was stunned. As I sat and thought about it, I felt it would be an honour to come to this wonderful retreat and actually be part of it. I had learnt so much by being here, and the general opinion of others who had attended the course was they found it beneficial as well as enjoyable. I went back to my room to have a shower and change, as tonight was our farewell dinner. I wanted to look good and feel good, as I would give my answer to my meditation teacher at dinner.

As it was the end of the course, the dinner was a lavish affair, and healthy was out, and in was the celebration of all things less so. On the table were bottles of wine, dips, chips, sweets, all things that were usually forbidden. We were being prepared to enter the outside world again. Everyone was sad as it was the end, but on a banner hanging on the wall was the saying, 'All good things must come to an end, but always remember, the end never comes'. I noticed Julie standing on her own, so I went over and talked to her. I asked if she would like to sit with me, as it was an open table with no name placements.

As we talked, she told me she had loved the course and hoped to come back to another one, in the future. I asked her how she was getting home, and she told me her husband and daughter were coming to pick her up, as she didn't have a driver's licence. "Julie, I would love to meet your Alice tomorrow; would you mind?" She said that would be fine with her. I felt in my heart I needed to see Alice and give her a hug, just to make physical contact with her. I didn't understand why, but the wanting was there.

We had a wonderful night, and amid all the laughter and fun I was able to give my teacher an answer. We ate all the forbidden foods that had been denied to us for the last fortnight. At the end of the night, the manager Sophia spoke and thanked everyone for attending the retreat and hoped we had a wonderful time, to which we all clapped and cheered.

Next, it was the meditation teacher's turn. On the course we only knew our peers as teachers but not by name, although he had told me to call him Joel when he asked me to join the team. Now he began his speech. "Good evening, everyone. I hope you have enjoyed your stay with us and will take home with you all you have learnt. I have a special announcement to make. Will you come forward please, Beth?" I didn't expect this, and felt humble, but managed to make my way to stand by Joel. "I have asked Beth to join our team and become a teacher on Overcoming Trauma. I don't know if you are aware of the ordeal that Beth has suffered. Can I quickly run through it, Beth?" I nodded my head.

"Beth's husband murdered their disabled daughter and because he worked at a funeral parlour, he put her body in a coffin with an elderly man who was about to be buried. Graves had to be dug up and bodies exhumed until they found Alice's remains." There were gasps of horror around the room. "For anybody to have to go through all this and come out with renewed self-esteem, then to go on to help other people, is nothing short of remarkable. Beth will tell you meditation helped her through this, so please find time each day to meditate, even if it is only ten minutes. Thank you, Beth, for agreeing to become a team member." Cheers rang out, and everyone came to me and offered their congratulations along with their condolences.

When I woke the next morning, something inside me made me feel excited. I couldn't work out what it would be. I went downstairs, this time to a normal breakfast of sausages, eggs, bacon and tomatoes. I had to admit I had really enjoyed the healthy eating, something I would pay more attention to in my everyday life. After breakfast, it was goodbyes and hugs all round, as everybody was bringing their suitcases down.

I saw Julie so went over to speak with her, to ask what time her family were arriving to pick her up. "They are here already; would you like to come and meet them?" I told her I would love to, so off we went to where the car was parked. Her husband was standing at the boot waiting to put her suitcase in. "Brent, I would like you to meet

Beth." We shook hands, and I told him I was pleased to meet him. I could see he was a lot older than Julie, but that she had found happiness was all that mattered. I did wonder if it was really love or if it was for security, but whatever it was, he apparently treated her well. That was all that mattered in the end.

Then we went to the passenger seat and opened the door. "Hi darling, this is Beth, my new friend. She wanted to meet you." Suddenly I now knew why I was excited; I was meeting Julie's Alice. I was shocked for a moment as there was a resemblance between the two Alices. "Hello Alice, it is nice to meet you. I met your mother here at the retreat and we have had a good time. Can I give you a hug?" I asked. She smiled and nodded. I leaned into the car and put my arms around her. I didn't want to let go as I felt a connection, but I had to be careful not to overwhelm her. "It was lovely to meet you, Alice. I hope one day we can meet again," I said with tears in my eyes. If only, dear child, you knew what your father had done to his two Alices, but no, you wouldn't want to know.

I thanked Julie for allowing me this privilege of hugging her daughter. "I will give you my phone number in case you would like to call me one day," she said. I accepted this and thanked her. As we said goodbye, I hugged her and whispered to myself, "This is not the last time we will meet."

Driving home from the retreat, I had a lot to think about. I had forgotten my memories for the last fortnight. Well, that wasn't quite right, as I had thought about John while I was there, but that was only at the beginning of the course, not for the last week. I really enjoyed myself; it was the first time I had let myself be there in the moment. To think I came away having been invited to be a teacher there. This was more than I could have thought possible! I wondered what my staff would say when I told them. It wasn't a full-time position, only when they ran courses on Overcoming Trauma. Then I would be required to attend for the duration of the course.

I hoped the teaching wouldn't interfere too much with my business. My work was not something I could hand on to my staff; although Bridget was a qualified case worker, people were particular about who they wanted to talk to. Perhaps if I let Bridget handle some of the new cases coming in, that might solve the problem. The ones who had dealt with me in the past always wanted to make appointments with me. A lot of my work was repeat business, and this is where the problem lay. When I knew a retreat course was coming up, I would tell my receptionist not to make bookings for me for the time I was going to be away.

It was nice to be back in my own home. I had taken the photo of Alice out of my suitcase and put it on my dresser in the bedroom. That made me think to call Sarah and James and let them know about Julie's Alice.

"Hi, Sarah. I've just come back from my retreat. It was great, I learnt a lot and you will never guess what: I have been offered a teacher's position at the retreat. Overcoming trauma is the subject I have been asked to speak on."

"Yes, you are certainly qualified to speak on that subject, Mother. Did you meet anyone exciting?"

I knew what Sarah meant, not what I was going to tell her. "Yes, I did, and it was a woman. I met your father's other lady friend, and she had a daughter to him. The daughter is compromised and is in a wheelchair. You will never guess what her name is – Alice! I met her and gave her a cuddle. She's a little like Alice; it was uncanny."

"You are joking, Mother. What made them call her Alice? I'm happy you were able to meet her; it will put your mind at rest."

"Apparently, your father wanted her to be called Alice. Remember she was born before our Alice was. I am wondering if he did really love my friend Alice and when she went missing, he wanted her memory to live on. He was not happy with me calling our daughter Alice, and now I know why, as he already had a daughter called Alice. I learnt a lot more about Phil and he was a proper sod. Thank goodness he is locked away where he can't do any more damage, unless he cottons on to a female prison officer."

"Mother, don't even go there; it is probable but hopefully not possible. I was wondering if you have heard from Toby since he shifted?"

I told her no; I hadn't heard anything. Why did she have to bring his name up? Now he would be in my brain. We said goodbye and then I had to call James and tell him what I had told Sarah.

The next morning when I turned up at work my staff were waiting to hear about the retreat. The first question they asked was whether I had met anyone interesting. I think they were hoping I was going to tell them I was romantically involved, so I disappointed them. I did tell them about meeting Julie and her daughter Alice. They were as surprised as I was. But I let them know I felt a bond with her when I cuddled her.

"Oh and just another little bit of news. I have been asked to join the staff at the retreat when they run seminars on overcoming trauma."

"Does that mean you won't be here much? Gosh, Beth, when are you going to slow down?"

I told them it was only when they decided to run a trauma class that I would have to attend. Now it was time for me to catch up on what was happening at work. I had two current appointments and was full for the rest of the week, so I was straight into it.

My first appointment was a reoccurring case. It never ceased to amaze me when you give people advice and they don't follow it, then wonder why things are not working out. It began with a marriage split-up. I had told my client to stay away from her ex, not to be in his face, but she was still so jealous she just couldn't stay away. She dropped letters in his mailbox every day, even leaving some pushed under his front door. I told her she was only making matters worse, that you can't force a person to love you. If he wanted a divorce, she should let him have it and she could get on with life. He was very good to her with money, halving everything with her, probably because he wanted to be rid of her, but she would not let go.

They had been married for ten years and thank

goodness there were no children involved, otherwise I don't know where it would have ended up. The ex-husband hadn't got another partner. He was possibly frightened in case he had to go through it all over again. I think she had been spoilt by him, and now that she didn't have him, she didn't know how to manage on her own.

Once again, I had to plead with her to stay away from his home and not leave letters in his mailbox. "He doesn't want you, so let him go, otherwise the police will become involved and take a court order out against you. You don't want that to happen, as then your name will be on the police register. Please listen to me and stay away from him. He doesn't love you any more and there is nothing you can do. Move away from here and start a new life. It is no good you coming back to me. I have given you all the advice I can, and it is up to you now. I'm sorry but this is our last appointment. Goodbye, Sandra, and all the best."

I hoped this was the last I saw of her. I told my receptionist not to make any more appointments for her, as there were more worthy cases out there waiting to be heard.

Part Two
John

John

John had never forgotten the day a stranger came to the door and said he was his father. Because his memory had never come back since the bombs were dropped, all he could remember was his name, as the last words he heard was someone calling him John. He didn't want to leave as he loved Beth and the new baby; this was now his life. He protested when his father came to take him away. He remembered them all standing at the door crying, and this was the last memory he had of them in person, but it was not the last time he thought about them.

John's new family home was in London in a council flat. When he was introduced to his mother, she smothered him with hugs and tears as she remembered the day they were out trying to buy food when the siren sounded. She had panicked and picked up her younger son and started to run back to the shelter only to see John running in the other direction. She had called to him to follow her, but it was too late, he was heading towards the bombing.

She had known that she would never see him again and the guilt never left her. So when they were reunited, she couldn't let go of him. John had to adapt to this new situation. His father got him a job in a timber factory as new homes were needed even while the war was still ongoing. No one knew how long it would last. Although he would have preferred to be at school rather than in factory work, the choice was not down to him. He had to fit in with his new family and their lives. His father was away most of the time as he was with the forces so had to go where he was posted. Thus, John became the father figure, and a lot was asked of him.

One day he was out walking when he passed a playing field and there were boys kicking a soccer ball around so he asked if he could join them. They were all having fun until the siren went. The boys thought they were safe being out on the open field with no buildings around to fall on them, and they kept playing. John knew what happened when a bomb hit, so he yelled for the boys to run. He took off but it was too late for the others, as a bomb struck the field.

The boys had disappeared, but where to? The blast had knocked John to the ground and left him dazed. As he came round, he got up and went to the huge hole left in the ground. There among the debris lay the twisted bodies of the boys he had been playing with. He let out a scream, but no one was around, as they had all run to the shelters. John sat and howled. He couldn't walk away and leave the bodies there alone, so he would wait until people came out of hiding.

John didn't know how long he sat there for, but he waited until he saw army men out looking to rescue people. He called out to them, and they came running. What confronted them looked like a mass grave. "What happened, why didn't they make it to a shelter?" someone asked. John explained that the boys had thought they were safe in an open field. "That's why there are sirens, to warn people to get to a shelter. Nowhere is safe when bombs are being dropped. It's too late for them, but you remember in future, when a siren goes, get to a shelter. How many boys were playing here?" he asked. When John told him there were thirteen lads, they were in disbelief. "My God, boy, this is your lucky day. Did you know the boys' names?" He told them he was just passing and asked to join them, so he couldn't help them.

"You go home. We will attend to this. Remember what you have been told: in future go to a shelter."

When John went home, he was really shaken up with what he had just witnessed. He sat in a chair and started to cry. He told his mother about playing in the field with the boys and then the bomb came. "What do you mean the bomb came?" she asked. John then had to explain what happened, that all the boys had died, and he was the only one that was left alive. His mother cuddled him and thanked God that he was spared.

"John, this has happened twice to you. I lost you once and suffered for two years, but thank God you are still with us. Please be careful and get to a shelter straight away when you hear a siren. My poor darling," she cried as she hung on to him. "I will call your boss and tell him you won't be at work for a couple of days, just so you can get over this."

John insisted he was okay. "It is better I go to work, as it will take my mind off what happened, otherwise I will sit here and cry all day." This his mother understood, and what John was saying was probably the right thing to do, so she agreed not to call his work.

That night when John went to bed, he had flashbacks of the last day he remembered: the siren had sounded and there was a loud explosion, everything was crumbling around him, he was swallowed up in dust and smoke. When he came to, he was in a makeshift tent being assessed by people in overalls. He didn't think they were doctors, perhaps something to do with the army. He could remember hearing someone saying, "This boy is a miracle. How he survived without being badly hurt beats all odds." Then there was nothing.

It had taken several days before he fully recovered as his lungs had consumed the dust and smoke. When he was asked where he was from, he couldn't remember so the only details they had were his name. A government employee had come to the medical tent with glass vials, so he offered to take John to his home as he was married and had a small child. This was how he came to be living at Beth's parents' home. So many children were separated from their parents during the air raids, and they were feared dead. The volunteers running the makeshift medical tents tried to record all the patients' details, in the hope that one day they might be reunited with their families. This is how his father finally found him. He went around all the medical tents to try to find if his son was still alive. He felt in his own heart that his first born had survived.

It took time for John to feel close to his own family. His mother fussed over him, and his brother took this personally, as he had enjoyed her undivided attention but now felt left out. Thus began the division between the two brothers, not from John's part but from Alex's. He was happy his brother had gone missing as he was pampered. Alex never put himself in John's shoes, so he had no empathy for him.

Now that John was working at the timber factory he didn't see much of Alex anyway, and he tried to stay out of his way. Their mother wanted her two sons to be friends, but she saw Alex driving a wedge between them, and this made her angry with him, which only made matters worse. John missed his little friend Beth, and he wished she was his sister. He did wonder how she was as he had good memories of their time together.

Three months on, John could see it wasn't working out living at home with his brother. He didn't want to upset the family, so he secretly enlisted in the army. The war was still raging so soldiers were needed, and the criteria for soldiers was different now to what it was at the beginning of the war. The original conscription age of twenty had been dropped to eighteen. Some who lied about their age were becoming soldiers at sixteen. These were the eager beavers that thought war was a game. John was just over sixteen so gave it a try and was accepted, as they were desperate for soldiers The initial training of twelve weeks had been reduced to six, due to the urgent need for combat-ready soldiers.

Next came the task of telling his workplace and his family. His boss accepted that it was his choice to defend his country. But it was a different story with his mother. She had lost him once, and then nearly for a second time, and didn't want to lose him again, so begged him not to go. His father understood as he was a soldier, but he was not all that happy. As for Alex, he was the only one who was happy that his brother was leaving home, as he would be an only child once again, and he could rule the household. John's mother saw a different side to her son Alex, and this frustrated her. She felt he had driven John out of the home, so she was going to teach him a lesson. He would soon learn of the mistake he had made by not making his brother welcome!

John had started his training and was passed as medically fit, so he was issued with a uniform, equipment and an identification tag. The basic training was discipline, fitness, the military march and to be able to follow commands and work together as a unit. British forces were deployed to various regions theatres of the war, but it was on the home front where soldiers were needed at that time. He was open to going overseas, as he had nothing to keep him in England. Besides it would be an experience. He had sort of lost family ties, and they had never been a priority for him, as his memory was still elusive. He really didn't know what family he actually belonged to in his heart, but he did miss Beth most of all. She had been just a little girl who he looked after, but he felt close to her.

For the next six weeks John worked hard on his fitness, and the regiment spent hours practising their marching skills. Discipline was crucial in the army, but this came easy to him as he could adapt to any circumstances. He liked to be with people and use their support to make final decisions. John fitted well into the army life, liking the regimental system, as they knew each day what their jobs were.

The East End was his first placement as this was where most of the bombing was occurring. His first deployment was with the medical team searching for survivors among the ruins. Volunteers were in short supply due to the loss of civilians, and people were frightened to leave the safety of the shelters. The first casualties John came across were a mother and a little girl, who had not made it back to the shelter and lay together among the rubble. He called for help, so a stretcher arrived, and the two bodies were carried to a makeshift morgue. The first thought that came to his mind was Beth; what if this had been her? It was enough to bring tears to his eyes, but he had to remind himself this was the first of many bodies he would find. Every day brought more heartache, as bodies lay among the ruins: the unlucky ones that never made it to safety in time.

One day John was summoned to headquarters to see his superior. He was asked to be seated. "John, you are a diligent worker. I noticed you didn't take your allocated days off, but instead you worked on. We are looking for men like you to join the forces that are being deployed to Normandy. Are you up for this?" He didn't have to think as he loved the army life. He knew the dangers, but they were not a deterrent. He had survived close calls twice, and he could do it again. He knew he had one more chance, as he remembered the saying 'third time lucky'.

"Yes, sir," was an instant reply.

"Take a week off to say goodbye to your loved ones, then report for duty."

John returned home to his family. Of course, his mother was most upset, especially when she knew he was being deployed overseas. "Why can't you stay in England? Why go abroad?" she pleaded. He explained soldiers were needed at strategic fighting points elsewhere, and he had volunteered. He didn't tell his mother what was involved as she would be upset. This was going to be a totally different battle, where bloodshed and death would be on the cards. He had been briefed on the amphibious landings and that the enemy would be waiting for them.

As luck would have it, his father was arriving today on leave, so they would all be together. One thing he did notice was a big difference in his brother's attitude, and Alex even asked John to explain about the army. John's father was a little hesitant when he learned of his son's deployment to Normandy, as he knew the Germans and how ruthless they were. He had the sense not to alarm his wife as to the dangers John was going to encounter.

The next couple of days came and went. John's father had returned to duty, so he felt it was time to go back to barracks. He missed his army mates and was ready to get on with the job.

Normandy, D-Day

BACK AT THE BARRACKS, there was extensive planning conducted under Operation Overlord, which John learnt was the codename for the upcoming Battle of Normandy. There were strategic decisions involved, planning, landing locations, logistics and the joining of Allied forces. For several days the regiment John was in underwent rigorous training exercises, including amphibious landings as well as combat drills in preparation for conditions they were going to face. They were briefed on their specific roles and had to study detailed maps, so they understood the terrain they were going to encounter. Each unit had to know their individual responsibilities.

Four days later, John along with his regiment were transported to embarkation points along the southern coast of England. This also involved moving vehicles and equipment as well as the soldiers. Here the forces boarded ships and landing craft and set off in convoys to specific landing zones on the Normandy coast. John's regiment was deployed in the landing craft with other regiments. The men were excited, but little did they know this was going to be the largest amphibious invasion in history. Today was 6 June 1944, known as D-Day, when the British forces and the Allies were to land on the French coast. The men knew airborne divisions were also deployed to help secure positions.

As the men left the landing crafts, gunfire rang out while they battled their way up the sandy beaches, facing intense resistance from German fortifications. Many men died even before they reached the beach, and many bodies were floating in the sea. But their training had instilled in them the understanding that they were there to do a job and they knew it wasn't going to be easy. Lives were going to be lost but they had an end goal, to defeat the Germans. John saw that some of his regiment had not made it, but he had to put this out of his mind. They had to overcome the obstacles ahead: mines and barbed wire as well as an onslaught of waiting machine-gun fire.

The massive invasion force, some 150,000 men in all, ensured success. Logistics and supply chains were crucial in ensuring the troops had the necessary ammunition, food and medical supplies. The Battle of Normandy, which began with the D-Day landings on 6 June, continued until 30 August. During this time, from 12 to 14 August 1944, Allied forces encircled and trapped a large number of German troops in the 'Falaise Pocket', resulting in heavy casualties for German forces. It was a decisive victory, causing the German garrison to surrender. John was right in the thick of the bloodied battle and was thankful he had survived, as many of his regiment had not made it, making it a bittersweet victory. So many lives were lost that the atmosphere was solemn. But the success of the Battle of Normandy paved the way for Allied advancement into occupied Western Europe and ultimately contributed to the defeat of Nazi Germany in May 1945.

John returned to England when his fighting days were over. He had lost some good friends but was thankful luck had been with him.

What to do next was something he had to think about. He had no idea where his future was going to take him, or what he wanted out of life. He would go home and see his family then decide. The war had come to an end in England, but the aftermath was a horrible reminder of what had happened. He thought perhaps if there was no work he would join the Civil Defence and help with the clean-up of the East End, as it was nearly non-existent. The Germans had set out to destroy England's main port areas and that's what they did.

When he arrived home, the government was asking for volunteers to help clean up the ruins. They would get minimal pay, but they desperately needed help to get the rebuilding under way. John had no commitments, so he volunteered until a job came up. His mother pleaded for him to return home to live, but John liked the company of the soldiers and stayed on in the army barracks. Also, it was an escape from his brother, although he had noticed a difference in him last time they met.

A colleague of John's sent a newspaper cutting to let him know there was a vacancy coming up at his workplace. It was in the assembly line at the Ford Motor Company at Trafford Park in Manchester. John telephoned to arrange an interview. It was known that soldiers that had served their country at war often got preference at job interviews as they were disciplined and very reliable. Hence this became his workplace, which he loved as he was working with fellow soldiers, so there was good camaraderie among the workers.

After work they all socialised together, and so began the pub crawls, dances and concerts to try to meet girls. They were young lads so what better time than now to let their hair down and start living? They had seen war and knew what could have been, having lost many friends. Sometimes their anger flared if they consumed too much alcohol, and it only took a bystander to say the wrong thing to precipitate an all-out brawl as the pent-up emotion emerged. John was the sensible one who could control his alcohol intake; he had to, as he was often the peacemaker of the group. Several times he had to haul his mates into line. He understood why the anger was there, as some people could not handle their war experience. They were a close-knit bunch of men.

Young women were on the radar now, so it was off to parties to find the girl of their dreams. John's best mate, Cory, had a sister called Rose and she would accompany them on some of their outings. She was a timid girl, not John's cup of tea as she was a bit prim and proper. He was more interested in someone who was outgoing and fun.

But because she was his best friend's sister, he tolerated her. He was even teamed up with her at some of the parties because she was left on her own. Rose was attracted to John and was always near him, as if she didn't want to let him out of her sight, hoping to catch his affections. She had told her mother she had met the man of her dreams, Cory's friend John, but she didn't think he liked her. Could she invite him for Sunday dinner? Then she could sit next to him.

On Sunday night John went to Cory's place. He wasn't all that excited because Rose would be there. He knew she liked him, but the feelings weren't reciprocated. But he didn't want to disappoint his friend. Rose met him at the door and took him through to the lounge to introduce him to her parents. Her mother was most polite, and the father was a quiet-spoken man.

"Cory had to go to the shops to get something for Mother. Come and sit with me in the lounge," Rose said. Reluctantly, John followed her then Rose asked him to sit on the settee. Next thing she parked herself beside him. They sat and looked at each other, with no words being exchanged, until Rose told him she liked him. He was lost for words and didn't know how to answer this, so he said the first thing that came to his mind, "I think you are a nice person." Rose seemed happy with this reply. Her mother came in and remarked how nice it was to see the two of them sitting together.

"Cory said you were in the army with him," Rose's mother said. "It must have been terrible to lose your friends. Cory doesn't talk much about the war, especially about when he went to Normandy. He must have seen some terrible things."

"Yes, it was quite horrifying at times, but even though we don't talk about it doesn't mean we don't think about it. It will always be with us."

"I think you are so brave," said Rose. Her mother saw the look in her daughter's eye and made up her mind that this was the man for Rose. He had a good job, was a respected veteran, and she could see plenty of potential in him. She didn't want her daughter to end up with a nobody; she had great aspirations for her, and John fitted the bill.

"Hi, I'm back. Where are you, John?" called Cory. He walked into the lounge and saw John sitting next to Rose. "Come with me, I'll rescue you from the girls," he said. John was relieved to be getting away from Rose and followed Cory out of the room. Rose then got up and went to her mother in tears. "Cory came and took John away. Why does he always interfere?"

"Now come on, Rose, they are best friends. I will talk to him later and tell him about your feelings for John."

"I love him, Mother. I don't want to lose him. Please help me to get him," she sobbed. Her mother promised she would work on it, but now it was time to serve dinner. She would sit John next to Rose, and that would keep her happy.

"Dinner's served," Rose announced as she knocked on Cory's door. He replied by saying they were coming. Cory's mother sat John next to Rose at the dinner table, just as she had planned it. As they ate their meal, Rose never took her eyes off John, and he felt uncomfortable. As soon as they were finished eating, Cory got up and asked John to go with him, and they left the room. This left Rose broken-hearted. "Dad, you talk to Cory and tell him not to take John away all the time."

"No, I can't do that; they are friends, and I'm not interfering."

"Dad, I love John. You tell Cory, right?"

Rose's father just shrugged his shoulders; he was used to a hen-pecked life, with very few rewards.

"Mum, tell Dad to talk to Cory," demanded Rose as she stalked off in a huff.

As John was leaving, he stopped off at the dining room to thank Cory's mother for a lovely dinner.

"That's fine, John. We will see you next Sunday, as Rose is going to cook dinner. She is looking forward to seeing you again. Bye for now!" and the door shut. Poor John, he didn't have a chance to make an excuse ... so next Sunday it was.

Work was important to John and he gave of his very best every day, which didn't go unnoticed by management. One day he was called into the office. "John, we like how you work, and the men all like you, so we would like to offer you the position of assembly manager. It will mean overseeing the men and making sure production flows smoothly. We see good potential in you. You will receive a good bonus and a pay increase." John was delighted and thanked the manager. He assured him he would do his best to keep the men happy and increase the overall output.

At the pub that night John shouted for his men and told them of his new position. They were all happy for him. Of course, when Cory told his family about John's new position, this cemented his standing in their eyes, especially Rose's. Now John was not just an ordinary worker but was a boss. How fitting, thought Rose's mother, when Rose and John married that would give Rose some standing in the community. Now there needed an all-out effort to get them together, and hopefully John would come to the party and start dating Rose.

It was Sunday, not that John was looking forward to it. If not for his friend Cory, he would have rung up and cancelled the dinner. When he arrived, he learnt Cory had been sent to the supermarket once again. This gave Rose her chance. "Come, John, we will go into the lounge," she suggested. John chose to sit in a chair instead of on the settee, which threw Rose's plans out the window.

"Cory told us you have a new position at the Ford Company, that of manager. I am really pleased for you, John."

"Yes, I have a lot more responsibility now, but I will handle it," he said. Rose told him she would like to be his girlfriend. John was shocked. He thought it was the guy that asked the girl, not the other way around. He had to think quickly. "I'm not really ready to have one girlfriend. I want to have a look around first. I haven't been out on many dates, so I want to be sure I pick the right girl," he said. Poor Rose, she was used to getting what she wanted, and this was not what she wanted to hear. "But I really like you, John. Please can we go out on a date?" she pleaded. To keep the peace, he agreed to take her to the movies the next Tuesday night.

Rose's mother came in and asked Rose to help with the dinner. When they went to the kitchen, Rose told her mother that she had to ask John for a date, as he never offered. "Really, Rose, that is quite pushy of you. You are meant to wait to be asked by the young man."

"I know, Mother, but I don't think he likes me much. He wants to date other girls, so what if he likes someone else and not me? I want him, Mother, and I'm going to get him," said a determined Rose. The claws were out! Once again at the table, John was put by Rose who demanded this to happen. As he was eating his dinner, John felt a hand on his thigh and was shocked, as it could only be one person. He moved it away, much to Rose's disappointment. It was a sad meal as Rose didn't get her way, so she sulked. When John was leaving, once again he was asked for Sunday dinner, but he got in first and said he had another engagement. Rose heard this and left the room crying.

As the weeks passed, John dated other girls and had a great time. He had taken Rose to the movies, but he wasn't much interested in her. One night she invited him to their home so he agreed, thinking the family would be there. But when he arrived there was only Rose and him. She had some alcohol ready, which he had never seen before at their home. She invited him into the lounge and brought the drinks in with her. She poured him a glass and one for herself then turned the telly on for them to watch. They were on the settee together.

As they watched the movie on telly, which was a love story, they had their drinks and snacks. Rose cuddled into John as the night went on, and he had never seen her quite so giggly. When she started to make a move on him, he started to worry and pulled away.

"Just a minute John, I want you to see something," and she jumped up from the settee and disappeared. When she came back, she was wearing her bra and knickers. As she came near John, she dropped her knickers and undid her bra and stood in front of him totally naked. John was speechless; he had never been this far with a female before. She took his hand and led him to her bedroom, where she started to undress him. "Come on, John, show me the man you are," she challenged him. Next thing his trousers and underwear were on the floor. Then he felt her clutching his manly parts, teasing him with her writhing body. She pulled him down on the bed and climbed on top of him. Before he knew what had happened, they were having sex. He didn't know if it was love or lust.

The alcohol had done its job, and now they were both lying in bed naked. John hadn't spoken a word; he was shocked with what had happened. He had to admit to himself Rose had a nice body. They must have dropped off to sleep because the next thing he heard a voice calling Rose, and before she answered, into the bedroom came her mother.

"Rose, what is going on here?" she asked. John felt so embarrassed he apologised profusely.

"I'll leave you to it," Rose's mother said as she left the room.

This was the beginning of the courtship between John and Rose. He felt he couldn't let Rose's family down, now that they knew they had bedded each other. She was the first person he had had sex with, but there was only that once, because now she had John, she played the innocent little girl. She came out of her shell and was good company, so John was not too unhappy with his decision. They courted for the next year, and then Rose told John they should get married, after which they could resume sex. This was an incentive for John, so he proposed to her. They planned to get married in the spring.

For the next six months wedding plans were being made, and Rose spent so much time trying to find the right dress. It was to be a big flashy affair, with Rose's family wanting to show off their daughter's great choice of a husband.

It was the night before the wedding and John's family had come to stay to celebrate their son's big day. His brother Alex was asked to be best man, so this pleased the family. John's parents were not flashy people, so when they met Rose's family, they felt quite humbled. They hoped John was going to be happy, as this was a totally different class of people he was mixing with. They seemed upper class from what they could make out, but they had only just met them, so perhaps this was a bit premature.

This was the first time they had met Rose, and they decided to wait before they passed judgement on her. She certainly had everything of the best, and as the night went on, they saw that she expected nothing but the best. They hoped John had made the right decision and that he would be happy. They knew he worked hard, which was why he had advanced so quickly up the ladder at the Ford Company.

John's mother wanted a word with him on her own, so she asked him to come with her to their hotel. He went to let Rose know this, but she had other ideas. John's mother told Rose she was going to steal him for an hour. "I'm sorry, but I have made other plans for John," she said. John's mother waited for John to say something, but he just stood there. "Well, they will have to wait because I'm taking John with me. Come on, John," and he followed his mother, leaving Rose standing. John's mother could see what lay ahead for John, if he didn't put his foot down right at the start.

John's mother had seen it all right there: Rose was a very spoilt young woman. She wanted the time to tell John she loved him dearly and had never got over the fact she left him that day the bomb was dropped. She just wanted this time to be with her special son, to be able to give him something she had saved for, unbeknown to any other family member. "John, I want you to have this watch, to always remember me. It is a token of my love for you." As John opened the box, there was the most beautiful gold watch with his name inscribed on the back. It read, 'To my darling son, John.' "Mother I can't accept this; it must have cost a fortune. Please take it back."

"No, John this is yours. I cried so many tears when I

thought I had lost you forever, and now I have been rewarded. It is my gift to you, my darling son."

John took his mother in his arms, and they cried together.

"I want to give you one word of advice, my son. Don't let Rose have all her own way; put your foot down when you need to, otherwise your marriage will not be a happy one." Secretly he knew what his mother meant, but after the wedding things would change. At times he wondered if he had made the right choice, but because Rose had bedded him in her parents' home, and they knew about it, it made things quite difficult. Was he marrying for the right reason or was it to save face? Only time would tell.

The wedding was quite an extravagant affair as Rose's parents wanted the best for their only daughter. Because Cory and John were ex-soldiers a lot of the guests were army men, so it was quite the military affair. As Alex was best man, this made his mother and father very happy.

John continued to do well at the Ford Motor Company. He became the production manager and led a large team of men, and he was well liked and respected. He had also become a father to two little girls, Beth (who was named after his little friend who he had looked after as a baby) and Shelley, and they were expecting their third child. John had told Rose about his earlier life, at least what he could remember of it, and that Beth meant a lot to him. He had cared for her and saw she was fed, as her mother was not a very reliable person, especially when it came to parenting. He always thought that if he had a daughter, he would like her to be named Elizabeth (Beth for short) as this kept his memories alive. He often wondered what sort of person she had grown into.

Rose had not been well with this baby, which concerned the doctors, so she was put in hospital for the last month of her pregnancy. Both parents took turns at looking after the girls until the baby was born. It was a boy, and there were health issues with him, but the seriousness of these would not be known until he was a little older. It was disappointing after having two healthy daughters, but this was how things could be, and the family had to move on.

Five years on

The Ford Motor Company had told John they wanted him to go to New Zealand to help pass on the valued work ethics he had instilled in his men in England. There was a little unrest with the New Zealand assembly line, so this was why he had been chosen. Also new technology had been introduced in Manchester and it was to be installed in the New Zealand plant, so he was the right person to oversee its introduction. This was a promotion for John, which came with a healthy pay rise. But it also meant a shift to a foreign country for the whole family. All costs would be met by the company and a home would be provided.

While he was excited, John did wonder how Rose and the family would feel, as it would be a big upheaval for everyone. Of course this was going to upset Rose's parents especially, as they were going to lose their grandchildren. After a lot of discussion with both families, it was decided that this was an opportunity that couldn't be turned down, as John had worked hard and deserved his promotion. Besides, it would be an excuse for the grandparents to travel abroad and visit them. John's two daughters, Beth and Shelley, were sad to leave their friends but were excited at the same time, as they were going to live in a new country, far away from England, almost on the other side of the world. It was going to be more difficult for Rose as she had to deal with their son Michael's health problems, but with John's new salary packet they could well afford home help.

There were tearful hugs all round as the families gathered at Heathrow to say their final goodbyes. They had a long flight ahead of them, with a stopover for four hours in Dubai. Michael had been given all his medication so it was hoped he would sleep most of the way. He would be starting his schooling in New Zealand as he had just turned five. The first Ford Company in New Zealand was located at Seaview, Lower Hutt near Wellington, and this was their destination. Everything was arranged at that end, with a home which was situated near schools and John's work. It had been stocked with all necessities to keep them going for a few days until they found their feet. They would feel jet-lagged for the first day or two, and John didn't have to start work for a week after his arrival. The company wanted him to have time to settle in and get the kids registered at schools. They were aware that there were problems with his son Michael.

The family's flight to their new country was a long haul. Michael's medication kept him calm, and he slept most of the way. The girls watched movies; they were easily entertained as it was all a big adventure to them. Their mother Rose was the one most affected; she felt a little on edge, wondering whether this was the right decision and if she would be able to manage Michael during his difficult times.

John noticed Rose was quiet, so he took her hand to reassure her all was going to be fine. A lot of stress had been put on her, and she was not a very strong person as she had been spoilt by her family, being the only daughter. Not to have her mother handy when things went wrong was a worry for Rose.

John often wondered if he had rushed into marriage as Rose had been his only girlfriend. He didn't find her very exciting, and he was sure there should have been more to marriage than what he was experiencing. She was willing to go to bed with him for the purpose of having children, but since Michael's birth she didn't seem to need or want sex any more. He felt he was still young and that was what marriage was all about: having fun in bed! But this wasn't to be. He could see she stressed out about their son, as his moods changed in the matter of a second without any warning. She was the one at home with him, so he was understanding when she voiced concern. John's way of overcoming what was missing at home was to bury himself in work.

After proceeding through customs, the family were met by John's boss who was there to welcome them. He introduced himself as Lyndon and he was going to drive them to their new home. Jet lag had set in and all they wanted to do was fall into bed. John thanked Lyndon and he arranged to call him in a couple of days. Lyndon would see a company car was dropped off at their home in the morning, so they could get out and familiarise themselves with their new surroundings.

Rose put Michael to bed, and he settled straight away, which was a miracle. The girls hadn't slept much on the plane and they felt jaded so off to bed they went. John opened a bottle of wine which had been left to welcome them and poured them both a glass. They sat on the settee and talked about their new life. Rose liked the house so that was a good start. John wanted his life to start on a totally new footing, so he had high hopes of making love to Rose tonight: a new country and a new life! He was in high spirits and as they climbed into bed he rolled over to cuddle her, hoping then to make love. But Rose was not in the mood, and she told him she didn't really care much for sex now that they had their family.

"But, Rose, we are young. This is what we are meant to be doing, having fun, being intimate with each other; that is what marriage is all about."

"I'm sorry, John, but I'm not that kind of person. We had sex when we had our babies, and that was enough for me. I didn't really enjoy it, but I wanted children, so I agreed."

John felt stunned and hurt. Was this going to be his life, was she not going to touch him or let him touch her? What was she thinking? Surely, she knew that a man needed to be loved and that sex was part of her duty as a wife. "Don't you like me touching your breasts and caressing you?" he asked. Rose's answer said it all. "My mother told me men expected sex, but she wouldn't let my father touch her after she had us children, as she didn't enjoy it either."

"Think back, Rose, to the night you invited me to your home, and we had some drinks. You stood in front of me naked, then you took me to bed. You were the first girl I had sex with, and I thought we would have many more nights where you would strip for me so we could have fun. But that hasn't happened since. What went wrong? We have never made sex fun. You just seem to grin and bear it to have children. But life is more than just having sex to make babies; it is to feel intimate with each other, to experiment with ways and means, to laugh and enjoy. Tell me why it just happened that once, Rose?"

"I wanted you John, but you didn't seem interested in me. You were dating other girls, and I didn't want to lose you, that's why I behaved badly that night. It was to snare you into bed with the hope that if my family caught us, you couldn't walk out. If I couldn't have you, no one else would."

"Did your mother know that was going to happen that night, Rose?"

"Yes, it was all prearranged. Mother thought you were a good catch, so we planned it."

"You told me that once we got married, we could carry on and have sex, and that is why I asked you to marry me, but the sex never happened. I'm disappointed with you, Rose. You married me under false pretences. Men want to have sex to feel close to their loved ones; they need it."

"Well, my father never had sex with my mother other than to have children, and he has survived."

"Yes, Rose, he survived, but what a sad hen-pecked creature he has become. Pity help me if I turn out looking like him. He is such a sad sack; can't you see that? He has nothing to look forward to in life, other than dying."

Now John knew where he stood: like mother like daughter. It had been ingrained in her right from the start. He was bitterly disappointed, but for the children's sake he would have to live in a loveless marriage. Work would be the substitute.

One year on

THE GIRLS WERE SETTLED into school and Michael was spending half a day at a special school. His concentration span wouldn't allow him to complete a full day as then the agitation would begin, so his mother would pick him up and take him home. She was tired every day, so her days were long. John could see this was a strain on her. They discussed getting a carer in three afternoons a week so Rose could have time out.

John's work was not easy going at the start, as he felt there was a little animosity towards him, and he put it down to the fact he was an outsider, a 'Pom'. He had to be patient and prove himself to the men and win their trust. It would take time but he would wait it out. He hoped they would give in before him. He could see why he was brought out, as the men needed proper guidance. Their old boss had let them rule the roost, but in his shift, he was the boss, which was something they would have to get used to. He liked his workers as they were willing men, but they had to learn there was only one decision maker and that was him. If things went wrong, then he was answerable.

John had the weekends off, and he would drive the family somewhere new each weekend, so they were finding places of interest. Sometimes John would park along Oriental Bay, and they would walk along the little beach there, especially on a sunny day.

Rose noticed little changes in Michael. He was becoming more aggressive as he grew older, but she didn't want to burden John with this, and instead she called her mother. This prompted them to come out to New Zealand for a visit. Unbeknown to John, this was arranged well before she broke the news to him. He didn't know how he would feel towards her mother now that he knew that she had helped her daughter deceive him. He felt sorry for her father as he would be putting up with the same misery as he was. What a waste of two good men.

On the day, the family were at the airport to meet Rose's parents. Their plane was late, so they had to fill in time until the plane touched down. Michael was getting upset and wanted to go home. John took him in hand and told him to be patient and that his grandparents were coming to stay. This didn't mean much to him. He started yelling, and people were looking at him, thinking he was being naughty. But once he started it just got worse, especially when he was told to behave. John was embarrassed so picked him up and took him outside, but Michael didn't stop; he screamed and tried to struggle out of John's arms.

This behaviour was a common occurrence, and John knew the only way to stop the screaming was to let Michael come out of it himself. The more attention you paid him, the more he seemed to play on it. Five minutes later he had calmed down, so John took him back into the terminal. The plane had landed so they had to wait until the grandparents cleared customs. It took another hour before they emerged.

Rose ran to her mother as she exited into the concourse, and they cried in each other's arms. Rose's father trailed along behind with the luggage, and as John looked at him, he could see the hangdog look on his face. He had never noticed it before and he wondered whether this might be him at his age. He hoped not, but it was quite on the cards! The girls rushed up to their grandad and hugged him. He looked at Michael and asked him for a cuddle, and slowly he came forward and obliged, but it was as if he couldn't remember him. They squashed into the car and drove home. There were presents all round and the chatter was rife. It was catch-up time.

The next morning once all the excitement was over, the grandmother called Michael over to sit on her knee. He refused and left the room. John went and fetched him and told him to do as was asked of him. The screaming started, for if he didn't want to do anything this was the result.

"Michael, come to Grandmother; I want to talk with

you. Tell me about your new school," she asked. As soon as school was mentioned he made his way over to her, but he wouldn't sit on her knee. "Do you like school? Have you made friends?" she asked. He nodded and smiled, but he wouldn't talk. The girls made up for him as they chattered away to their grandparents about their new school. They said they loved New Zealand and the kids at school were friendly, and the weather was much better here. Also, it wasn't as busy as England.

"You should see their parliament. It's like a beehive, and that's what it is called. It is nothing like Buckingham Palace. It is a different world out here, so far away from any other country. Our nearest neighbour is Australia and you either have to fly or cruise there."

When the in-laws' stay was nearing an end, John was relieved. He had seen a different side to his mother in-law. She wasn't a warm person, and he felt pity for her husband. He was just a commodity that came along with her. He noticed there was no affection between them, no touching or even a kiss. John decided at that moment he would show a little more affection to Rose in front of her parents, just to see the reaction.

After dinner Rose sat on the settee, so John sat beside her and put his hand on her knee. Later he moved his arm up and put it around her, pulling her closer to him. The mother shifted her gaze away from them, and it wasn't long before she announced she was off to bed. The father trotted along after her. "Why did you do that for in front of Mother? She doesn't approve of displays like that," spat out Rose.

"What a pity. Your father looks like he could do with a bit of affection paid towards him. He is a sad-looking man. As I have said before on several occasions, I hope I don't look like him at his age." With this Rose got up and announced she was off to bed: like mother, like daughter.

John's loveless life

As the years passed, John's home life was no different. Rose still hadn't come around to his way of thinking, that sex was part of married life, and a man needed to feel wanted. He felt he was just there to make the money to provide the family with what they needed, with no rewards for him!

The one thing that had changed was Michael was no longer living with them. Over the years his violence had worsened, so he was now in a home for young adults who were a danger to society. This made life easier for Rose and the girls. Beth was working as a clerk for an accounting firm, and Shelley was a wardrobe seamstress for a production company. They loved living in New Zealand and even forgot their early lives in England. But not Rose, who missed her mother. Sadly, both lots of parents had passed away as now Rose and John had reached their late fifties.

Every Sunday, as a family they went to visit Michael, but he was still disruptive and out of sorts, so some visits were very short.

At the Ford Company, the assembly line production had risen substantially with John at the helm. He had won out in the end, and the men fell into line and enjoyed working under him, as things got done with no hiccups. He had a knack of bringing the best out of his workers, and this was reflected in the work output. Therefore, their wages rose according to production. On a Friday after work John would take his men to the local pub and shout for them. This was his social outing, as Rose didn't ever want to socialise. She was a homebody, very boring, but a loving mother to her daughters.

Rose had not been feeling well lately but elected not to tell John. Although he noticed she was quieter than usual, he put it down to the fact she was old before her time, a mirror image of her mother. One night she woke in terrible pain, so he called the ambulance, and she was taken to hospital. After tests, the results showed cancer of the stomach. It was too far gone for any treatment so all they could do was keep her comfortable.

"How long have you been unwell?" the doctor asked Rose. When she told him it was just under a year, John interrupted. "Why didn't you tell me?" The doctor told her if she had come sooner, they could have treated her, but now it was too late. John was angry she had hidden her sickness from him, and apart from not being a loving wife he felt she had let him down completely. If not for Beth and Shelley, he felt his life had been wasted. He had provided well for his family over the years and now he felt betrayed.

For Rose not to share her state of ill health with him was the end. When he looked back over his life, it was sad and empty. He decided he would have to talk to his daughters about marriage, because if Rose had instilled in them what was instilled in her by her mother, then their marriages would be doomed from the onset. Now it was just a matter of time before Rose passed away. Her last wish to John was her ashes had to go back to England, to her homeland. The wait was short, as two days later her life ended.

After a long flight, the plane had finally landed at Heathrow. John's brother Alex and his family were meeting him at the airport and taking him to their home. He was there to carry out Rose's wishes, to bring her ashes home to England. They were in his suitcase.

He hadn't met Alex's wife or family as he had never returned to England. He hoped his brother's life was more exciting than his. After the introductions, it didn't take long for John to notice Alex's life was the total opposite to his. His wife took his hand, and they walked hand in hand to the car. He could never remember Rose taking his hand on her terms; it only happened when he initiated it.

Alex had two children, a pigeon pair. They seemed a happy family as there was plenty of laughter. On arrival at Alex's home a bottle of champagne was opened to celebrate his return. They all sat round and John was bamboozled with questions about New Zealand. He felt welcomed in this warm environment. It was certainly a huge contrast to his life.

Over the next couple of days, Alex drove John to Manchester as this was where Rose asked for her ashes to be sprinkled. She hadn't specified where, so he was left in the dark. As they drove past where she used to live, there was a park nearby, so he asked Alex to stop. He took out the scatter box and opened the lid and let her ashes fly freely to where they settled. He hoped she would be happy.

John managed to have a heart-to-heart talk with Alex about his marriage, and Alex was saddened by what he was told. He said he couldn't complain about his relationship as they were as much in love today as at the beginning and their sex life was great, even to this day.

After a week with Alex, John hired a rental car to drive to London, as he wanted to see the transformation of the East End. It had been a disaster zone when he left, so he was keen to see it with his own eyes. He had seen photos. He was looking forward to going back to his old stamping grounds. Suddenly, his thoughts went to Beth: what had happened to her, was she still in the area or had she left like so many others? If she had got married, she would have a different name, and he had no idea what that would be. Was her life so different to his? He hoped she was happy and that she didn't feel it was wasted like his. He had a successful working life but that is as far as it went.

His first impression as he drove into the East End was one of bewilderment. The ruins had disappeared and a whole new landscape had emerged. He couldn't get over the rows upon rows of council flats that were everywhere. It didn't matter in what direction he looked, they were still there. But of course, they were built to house the people after the war, as hardly any homes were left standing. The wharf area and the shipyards were back functioning, and it was as if nothing had happened. The odd remnant remained, just to remind people that the Second World War had in fact happened. He found a quaint little pub so booked in for a few days. It wasn't far from where he remembered Beth had lived.

John had spent two days driving around and now it was time to walk the street to see if anyone knew of a Beth Collins. It was a long shot, but miracles were known to have happened and if not, then it would be just another chapter in his sad life. The first day brought no joy, but he had just walked two of the ten main streets, so there was plenty of time yet he told himself. It was day three that brought a little glimmer of hope. A man he spoke with thought he knew the name Beth Collins because of the murder trial. He tried to think, but he was sure it was a Beth Collins whose daughter was murdered by her own father.

John was shocked upon hearing this news. His life was nowhere as tragic as that. What had Beth been through? He didn't want to continue looking; he just wanted to go back to the pub to process what he had been told. He lay on the bed trying to think what age she would be now. If he was fifty-nine then she would be ten years younger, making her around forty-nine.

In the morning he continued on his mission to find

Beth, and hoped something concrete would come out of the day. As he tramped the streets, he came across a chemist shop, so decided to ask if they knew a Beth Collins. It was worth a try! The only Beth they knew was Beth Trainor who had a business in the side street off the main street, at number 19. As soon as John mentioned a murder, they said yes, that was the same Beth. He thanked them as he left the shop.

Tears flowed as he wondered whether he had finally found her. Was this his 'little Beth'? He hoped so. But he had to think carefully about his next move. Perhaps he should go and fetch the car and park it outside her business and wait. He had no idea what she looked like, as she was just a little kid when he last saw her. Yes, he would do this.

At 5.30pm he saw three people emerge from the office, one a younger girl and there were two older women. One was dressed in a lovely floral dress and the other was dressed more businesslike. If this was Beth's office, then she was sure to be the businesslike one. It was the other one that took his eye. He wound down his window, hoping to hear someone speak. "I'll see you both in the morning. Don't be late," the one in the floral dress was laughing as she called to the other two. So, this must be Beth! John was beside himself. She looked lovely and she seemed to be a happy person. Could his luck change?

John sat in the car for a long time and suddenly the streetlights came on. When he looked at his watch it was seven o'clock. He wished he could stay there all night to be there for her in the morning, but that couldn't happen.

If the police were on their beat and found him parked there all night, he would probably be arrested.

That night he went to bed a contented man and had a wonderful sleep. In fact, too wonderful, as when he woke it was 9.30. "Damn, I've missed her. She will be at work now," he scolded himself. He wanted to be at her office at eight o'clock when she arrived at work, but no, that would not be happening. He had a bite to eat then got into his car and drove to her office, but there were no parks left so he had to park in the next street. He walked back to the office and stood outside. He was shaking with excitement; what would he do next? There was only one thing to do, straighten up and go on.

John walked into the office and up to the reception desk. "I'm here to see Beth," he said to the young receptionist.

"Do you have an appointment?"

"No, I'm sorry I haven't."

"Oh, you have just missed her. She has gone out for the day."

John stood there dazed. "Can I leave a message for her?" he asked. The receptionist said that would be fine, so she gave him a pad to write on. "No, I'll leave a verbal message. Could you please tell her that John, her old babysitter, called in." She thanked John and assured him Beth would get the message in the morning. With this he left the office feeling both excited and disappointed. "If only I hadn't slept in, I would be talking with her by now," he told himself. He made sure he went to bed early, so he didn't oversleep. But an early night to bed left him time to think about Beth. He wondered what he was going to find out tomorrow. He felt excited. He thought they could be good friends. They had so much to learn about each other. Would he tell her about his loveless marriage? No, that would be going too far! But what of her life? He remembered the man had said something about a murder. Tomorrow was the day he had waited for; all would be revealed.

My mystery visitor

WHEN I ARRIVED at my office the next morning my receptionist told me she had a message for me. I was running a little late, so my staff had everything ready to go. "Beth, a nice man called in yesterday just after you left. He told me to tell you his name was John, and that he was your old babysitter." I could have been knocked over by a feather.

"Are you sure that's what he said? What else did he say?"

"That's all he said then he left."

"Oh my God, I can't believe it. What did he look like?"

"He was a good-looking man, very upright, a bit older than you, I would think."

I had to sit down; my eyes filled up with tears. "Are you okay?" she asked. What could I say? This was my past becoming my present. Not many days had gone by that I didn't think about John, and when I was at my worst, he was the first person I thought of, and now he was here, but where?

I opened the office door and stood on the street looking up and down, but no one was in sight. I rushed back in and yelled at my receptionist, "Did he say he was coming back or where he was staying? He must have said something other than what you told me?"

"No, Beth, what I told you was all he said, then he left. He seemed surprised you weren't in. I thought he must have had an appointment with you, and you had forgotten, as he came straight up and asked to see you."

I was angry and devastated at the thought of perhaps not being able to see him. The tears flowed, and my staff had never seen me so emotional. "What is wrong, Beth?" they asked as they came up and hugged me. I couldn't speak and I wanted to be on my own, so I went into my office, closed the door and continued to weep.

I was disturbed by a knock on the door. Oh my God, how long have I been crying for? Then I remembered I had an appointment at 11.30, so this must be it. "Just a moment," I called as I tried to pull myself together. What would that person think? My eyes were red and swollen, and I was in a terrible state, then I looked at the clock on my desk: one o'clock. But what about my 11.30 appointment? How did all that time pass without me knowing?

There was another knock at the door. I have to answer it, I told myself, so I took a deep breath and opened it. There before me stood a stranger. Why didn't my staff tell him I was busy? They knew I was upset. Suddenly a voice said, "Hello, Beth, I'm John." I stood there dumbfounded. Here was the reason I was upset, and what I was making myself a bag of misery over. I felt paralysed; I couldn't say anything. My voice had gone and all I did was stand and stare at him.

"It's okay, Beth, I'm not a ghost, I'm John."

I rushed at him and held on for grim death. This time I wasn't going to let him go. When I recovered, I stepped back and apologised for my irrational behaviour.

"That's the sort of welcome that doesn't need an apology. How are you, Beth? I've thought about you many times over the years wondering what happened to you, and what sort of life you have led, and now I have found you. How wonderful is that?"

Now it was my turn to say something sensible. "When I found out you had called in yesterday and I had missed you, suddenly a grey cloud appeared, and it rained many tears. Just look at me, John, I have been bawling my eyes out thinking I was never going to have the chance of meeting you. I'm so sorry, I must look frightful. Please forgive me."

Then there was silence while we both stood looking at each other. Suddenly, we burst out laughing. It was as if we knew what each other was thinking. "Come here you daft girl," John said as he held out his arms. I fell into them effortlessly. "Right, this is not the place for discussions. You're busy so would you like to come to the Angler's Arms after work and have dinner with me?" With this he stood up and took my hand. "I'll see you just after 5.30. I can't wait to discuss our lives. Bye till then," and he let my hand go and left.

Now that John had gone, it was time for me to apologise to my staff for my earlier performance. I felt I had let myself down. "I'm sorry for my behaviour. It was unprofessional of me, of all people. I thought I had missed the chance to meet John, after all these years. He lived with us during the war, and he looked after me when I was a child. Then one day his father came and took him away. We lost touch but I have never forgotten him; he has been in my thoughts all these years. That's why I lost it when I thought I would never have the chance to see him ever again. I'm so sorry! By the way, what happened to my 11.30 appointment?"

"We knew you were upset so we rescheduled it. The client didn't mind."

My next two appointments were a blur as I couldn't concentrate. My brain was wired to John. I was so excited I couldn't wait for 5.30 so I finished a little earlier. I gave my staff the time off on pay. I decided to duck home and freshen up. I had to bathe my swollen eyes to try to remove the puffiness. Gosh, I was a mess! Never mind, the make-up hid a multitude of sins. And now I was off onto the next exciting part of my life. It had been four years since Toby moved, and although my feelings for him were still there they were dimming. I realised I couldn't hold on to a dream that wasn't going to go anywhere. It was hard to let go, but one had to be sensible about things that had no future. I could not give up on him completely, as he had a piece of my heart.

I was excited at meeting John. We had so much to talk about, but where would we start? My thoughts raced: was he married, did he have a family, where did he live…? Soon I was about to find the answers. I drove into the Angler's Arms carpark and as I walked into the lounge bar there was John seated at a table. He waved for me to come and join him and as I came near, he got up and pulled out a chair for me. "Very gentlemanly," I thought to myself. I sat down and we looked at each other and smiled. John asked me if I would like a drink, so I chose a chardonnay, and he came back with a pint of beer for himself.

I was keen to know if he was married so this was my first question. "John, I have to ask you, I know I'm being nosey, but are you married?"

"That is the reason I am here back in England. My wife wanted her ashes brought back to her homeland."

"What do you mean, her homeland?" I asked. It was then I learnt he lived in New Zealand, and he was back to spread his wife's ashes. So, he didn't live in England, which was a shock. He must have loved his wife to fly all this way to bring her ashes back, so I had to ask. "Did you have a happy marriage, John?" There was some hesitation before he answered. "To be truthful, Beth, I rushed into marriage. Rose was my first girlfriend; she was my best friend's sister. I had just come back from fighting in Normandy and I met Rose. Her family sort of pushed for us to be together. We had three children, Beth, Shelley and Michael, but sadly my marriage was lacking in love. After Rose had our children that was the end of any intimacy between us. So no, my marriage wasn't what I wanted from life, but perhaps I had expected too much. I never felt wanted, that was my greatest regret, just to feel close to someone, but sadly it never happened."

"Why did you stay together?"

John told me about his son Michael. He felt it was his duty to be there to help Rose cope, as he was not an easy child. As Michael grew older, he became more violent, so John couldn't leave. This was a plus in my book as he obviously faced his responsibilities. Not like someone else I knew.

"I see you called your eldest daughter Beth. Why?" John explained that he had told his wife about me, and he wanted his first child if it was a daughter to be called Beth.

All those years I spent wondering if John's life was better than mine … now I knew.

Now it was John's turn, so he mirrored my questions. "Are you married Beth?"

Where would I start and how would I finish as I was about to relive my nightmare. I told John my life's story and I noticed at times there were tears in his eyes. He listened intently as I drew him into my terrifying ordeal. My story verged on a horror story.

John reached over and took my hand; his eyes were filled with tears. "All through my life I wondered what sort of life you had. My God, Beth, I'm so sorry. How you have come out of this defies all odds. Your life would be everyone's worst fear. Dare I ask, are you in a relationship at the moment?"

It was my time to hesitate, but I wasn't going to pretend. "The detective on my husband's case was a young man who was the most thoughtful, considerate person I had ever met. He was very respectful, perhaps too much so. I fell in love with him, and I even told him of my feelings. He was flattered, but sadly he was also married, so it couldn't go anywhere. Also, there was the age difference. He shifted away four years ago, and we haven't had any contact, but with him went a piece of my heart. So that's my life in a nutshell … heartbreak and heartache!"

John squeezed my hand. "You know, Beth, you were just a child when I was taken away from your family, but I still held those memories of you. When I met my real family, I always wished you were my little sister. I would have traded my brother for you. Life is so strange. Why did we worry about each other's life?

"Let's order our meal and finish our drinks so we can recharge our glasses."

While we were waiting for our food to arrive, we looked at each other, absorbing what we had learnt, and as it turned out, neither of us had the life we had hoped for. I studied John's face. He had been a good-looking guy and now age was starting to show, but he had smiling eyes that sent out a warmth that I felt. What a shame he hadn't experienced a loving relationship. I had a sudden thought: was he summing me up as I was him? It was as if we were both lost souls.

Our meals arrived so our discussion turned to food. We learnt about each other's palate, which was amazing as we both love to experiment by trying new dishes and tastes. Neither were great dessert fans and we'd both rather settle for a cheese board. The more we learnt about each other the more alike we seemed to be. It was a strange feeling, I felt we had known each other all our lives …but the truth is …we had!

John went on to tell me about his life after being taken away from us, how he survived another bomb attack where a group of boys died. He talked about his new family, his time serving his country at war, and his promotion within the Ford Company which led to his shift to New Zealand. We had so much catching up to do, but the night slipped by so quickly. It wasn't until time was called for the patrons to leave as the pub was closing that we realised how late it really was.

"I'll walk you to your car and make sure you are safe," John said as he got up from the table. We walked to the car and when I unlocked it he opened the door for me. As I climbed in, he said in a whisper, "Thank you for a wonderful night, Beth, it was the best ever," then he shut the door. I then realised we hadn't arranged to meet again. I didn't know how long he was going to be in England as we never got around to discussing that.

"Please come to my home tomorrow night, John, and I will cook you a home-made dinner."

That night as I lay in bed so many things swirled around in my head. We both had sad stories to tell, and there didn't seem to be a bright light in either of our lives, and to think we worried about each other for all those years. Now, forty-four years on we were sharing our life stories. All through my life I wondered whether John's life was better than mine. I compared them thinking his wouldn't be as bad, and perhaps it wasn't, but happiness had eluded him, as it had me. Here we were both unattached. John's life was in New Zealand and mine was in England, so how much further apart could we be?

The next day at work I told my staff about John's life and how well we got on together and how much I enjoyed our night. "Do you think there could be anything between the two of you?" they asked. I stopped in my steps. Yes, I enjoyed his company, and he was polite and respectful, but he was a lot older than me.

While we were talking someone came into the office. I looked up and there stood John. "Hi, how are you today?" I asked. For a moment I thought something had happened, but he laughingly told me I hadn't given him my address, so how could he come for dinner tonight? We all laughed, and he jokingly said, "Perhaps you didn't want me to come." Once I gave him my home address, he thanked me and said he would see me later.

"He seems a really nice guy, Beth, such a lovely smile," my receptionist commented. Yes, I had to agree, he had a warmth about him that was infectious.

My first appointment today was made over the phone to my receptionist, who at the time commented that the voice was that of a younger person. When my client arrived, I was surprised to see a young girl in a college uniform. Her name was Amber so after introductions I asked how I could be of help. She seemed a little embarrassed, so I put her at ease by telling her I handled many different cases, so nothing surprised me.

"I don't know how to tell my parents that I prefer girls

to boys. I have a girlfriend who feels the same towards me and we go out together. My parents think we are just good friends. I have heard my parents talking about same-sex marriages as abnormal and disgusting. I have tried going out with boys, but I'm not interested," she said.

"How old are you, Amber?"

She said she was eighteen and was head girl at Xavier College, which surprised me as I would have put her at sixteen. "As you are an adult you will know what your sexual feelings are telling you. Are you in a sexual relationship with your friend at the moment?"

Amber nodded.

"You should go with what you feel comfortable with. Have you had a bad experience with the opposite sex to make you feel this way?"

She said no, she just didn't have any feelings towards them.

"Your parents may not like what they are going to hear, but it is your life. Sometimes this can put pressure on the family and may cause a split, but this is usually short lived. How do you think your family will handle this?"

"I was wondering if you could tell them, as I am frightened of what they will do because they are really strict. They are upper class so this would be a big disappointment for them. Their social standing matters to them, which is why I can't tell them. They have tried to match me up with the head boy at St Patrick's College. He is keen, but I am not, and my parents are angry with me. Please can you help me?"

I could see Amber was nearly at her wits' end over this predicament, so I agreed to speak with her parents. We made an appointment for them to come and see me. I had a feeling that this case was not going to be easy, because dealing with people who put their status first were very hard indeed. They couldn't cope with issues that would reduce their popularity among their peers, even at the expense of their families. But this was why I loved my work; if I could help one person a day who had no one beside them, then I felt I was contributing to humanity!

I was taking the afternoon off to prepare a nice dinner for John, so the office was my staff's for the rest of the day.

A night to remember

After finishing my food shopping, I stopped off at the store and bought two bottles of wine and a bottle of whisky, in case John didn't drink wine. As this was only our second meeting, I wasn't sure what he liked to drink, apart from beer. I spent the whole afternoon preparing the dinner. Now it was time for me to change into something nice as John would be here soon. I chose a colourful dress that I felt comfortable in, as I felt it reflected my personality. I fluffed around tidying up, all unnecessary of course, but it was a time filler. I had to confess I was nervous.

When the doorbell rang, I called for John to come on in. He looked smart in a dress shirt and tie. Before I could say anything, he said, "You look lovely tonight, Beth. You suit bright colours; they make you look happy." I thanked him for his compliment, the first for many years, but I would take it.

"I was going to pay you a compliment, but you beat me to it."

He put a bottle of wine and a box of chocolates on the table. "Just a little thank you," he said. "You haven't eaten yet, it might be a bit premature," I joked. He walked over to a photo and asked, "Is this your daughter you lost?"

"Yes, that is Alice. She was a lovely girl in spite of her disability. We all loved her, except Phil. She was a determined young lady who knew where she was going in life, but sadly…"

"I'm sorry, Beth, your life has thrown some severe challenges at you, but look at you now, you have your own successful business. You are certainly resilient."

"I've had to be, John. I could have gone the other way, but I didn't want my past to ruin my future. I hated my husband because he hurt me in so many ways, some I haven't told you about. He was the biggest mistake of my life. So I have since buried myself in work helping others who need someone there for them."

"You are a real trooper, Beth, you deserve better, and one day it will happen."

"Right, you open the wine while I see to the dinner," I ordered.

After we had eaten, and the dishes were cleared, we started on the cheese platter. Dinner had gone well; John was full of praise. We were on our second bottle of wine and were both quite relaxed. "You know Beth, this is what I missed, the companionship of sitting and talking over a wine. I never experienced these comforting times in all the years I was married."

"Did you not talk to Rose about feeling wanted?" I asked. It was then he opened up about what Rose's mother had instilled in her about marriage, so she carried on the tradition. "Sex was just to get babies, then it was over."

"Gosh, we are a sad pair, John. To think all our lives we worried how the other was managing, and as it turned out, one was as miserable as the other. You have to laugh otherwise you'd cry. John looked at me and shook his head. "You are very strong, Beth. What a shame you never met a person who saw all your wonderful attributes. In saying that, you are still young enough to find that person. He is out there somewhere."

As the night progressed, we seemed to get closer to each other on the settee. I felt an arm go around me. I was comfortable, so I snuggled into John. Silence reigned, neither wanting to say anything. This was the first time in years I felt an attraction to the opposite sex. He was kind and filled me with warmth; what was happening to me? Then I felt a kiss placed on my cheek and as I turned to face him, I noticed tears in his eyes. That was the end; my heart was touched. I reached up and kissed his lips. He smiled as he encased me in his arms. What came next was a shock to us both. We hurriedly undressed and lay on the floor touching and kissing each other and then made love. It was a magical moment for both of us. Neither of us spoke; we just lay there like teenagers who had met for a sexual rendezvous. I reached for the fur rug off the settee and covered ourselves, and there we spent the night.

When I woke in the morning, I was a little perplexed. This was not premeditated sex; it was a moment in time when something unpredictable happened. It had bolted out of the blue and was amazing! My mind turned to John: what was he thinking? I was too embarrassed to ask, but I didn't have to. "Thank you, Beth, for the most incredible night of my life. This is what I dreamt love would be like, and now I know."

We both laughed at our situation: two grown-ups making love on the lounge floor and spending the night there … how classic was that? I pulled on some clothes, enough to get me to the bathroom to have a shower. I called to John that he could shower after me. While feeling the water run over my body, happiness overcame me. I hadn't experienced these feelings for years; in fact I had forgotten how amazing it was. Then I wondered, where does this go from here? While John was in the shower I made breakfast. We needed to eat to replace some of the energy that was lost last night. As he came out from the shower I had to look the other way; again embarrassment overcame me. We were older adults, but we behaved as if we were young again. But then we had both missed out on our younger lovemaking years … so why worry?

Quietness settled over the breakfast table, then our eyes met, and we burst into laughter. It was one way of covering up our embarrassment until I spoke. "John I can't believe what happened last night, but whatever it was, it was great. It was just an ordinary situation that ballooned into a naked romping session. Are you okay with what happened, because today I feel embarrassed?"

"My dear Beth, don't feel embarrassed. What happened

was not planned. It is what the night led up to. We were comfortable with each other, then our feelings got the better of us and we had wonderful sex. I had almost forgotten about that part of life, not in my brain, but in my body, so I was pleasantly surprised that everything worked, and I didn't let you down. But having a willing partner sets the scene for everything to flow perfectly, so thank you. Please don't have any regrets about last night as it meant the world to me; you made me a happy man! I hope you feel the same."

I nodded and smiled. "What are you going to do today?" I asked. Then I thought about how much longer he had before he left England, as we hadn't got around to discussing that, so I asked him.

"I'm going to stay with a friend for two nights, then I will come back and say goodbye before I leave to stay with my brother before I fly out of Heathrow."

"Oh, are you leaving for your friend's today?"

"Yes, I have made arrangements so I will see you in two days' time."

My heart sank. Two days was a long time. I walked to the car with him. I was sad but tried to hide my feelings. He leaned over and kissed me and thanked me for a wonderful night. As he was getting into the car, I couldn't hold back. "I'll miss you," I called as I walked back to my house, tears filling my eyes.

I remembered that later I had an appointment with Amber's parents. I was prepared for the backlash that would come, when they found out about their daughter's secret. If their status meant more to them than their daughter's wellbeing, I was going to have a battle on my hands, as I was fighting for Amber. For goodness' sake, she was a head prefect of a college. Shouldn't they be happy for that alone?

The time had arrived and so had Amber's parents. They came into my office wondering why they were there. "I had a visit from Amber. She was upset because she felt she couldn't discuss her problem with you, so she asked me if I would break the news to you."

"What news, what problem? She knows we are here for her, so why did she come to you?"

"Amber didn't know how receptive you would be. I won't beat about the bush: she wants you to know she is a lesbian; she has a partner who she loves..."

"What do you mean she's a lesbian? She can't be; she's a head girl. How can she be like that?" shouted her mother.

"I'm sorry but she is eighteen, an adult, so she is free to choose her own friends. This is why she couldn't tell you as she knew how you would react."

"Our friend's son is interested in her. He is a good catch, and we are trying to match them up."

"No, you can't make arrangements for her. She knows what she wants, so you will just have to accept it."

"What will our friends say? They will be devastated. No this cannot happen. What would make her think she is like that? No, she is all mixed up! Say something Derek, don't just sit there. Your daughter thinks she is a lesbian."

Poor Derek, either he was in shock, or it wasn't such a big deal to him. "I don't like the idea, but if she has that tendency what can we do?" he answered.

"Of course we can do something. We will take her to a psychologist and get her assessed. She doesn't know her own mind."

"I'm sorry, Amber has made it quite clear what she wants in life. She has a girlfriend and nothing you can do will change anything. She is of age to make her own choices."

"You sound as if you accept her thinking, but what has it got to do with you?"

"Amber came to me for help. I listened to her, and I agreed with her. As an adult she can make her own choices, and you cannot force her to like the opposite sex if she is not interested. I'm sorry, but you just have to face the fact that your daughter is a lesbian. Please don't let this issue come between you. You are lucky to have such a talented daughter. I lost my daughter, and I live with that every day. Don't let this happen to you."

The parents got up and headed to the door without a word. Poor Amber, she would cop it tonight.

After I closed the office, I didn't want to go home to an empty house, as memories of the previous night lingered in my mind. I went back to the Angler's Arms and sat in the same seat as John and I sat at two night earlier. I ordered a wine and reminisced. It was just nice to see people enjoying themselves. The barmaid came over to me. "Are you on your own tonight? Where is your man? I remember you from two nights ago."

"Oh, he's out of town for a couple of days," I told her. When I had finished my wine, I left and drove home. As I walked in the door I started to laugh. I couldn't believe what went on here last night; it was like a den of iniquity. How did it happen? I had just met John, but I felt we had been friends forever … and we were! The night was lonely. I had lived on my own all these years and it never bothered me, so why now? What was going to happen when John flew back to New Zealand? We would be a world apart.

The next morning at the office a call came through for me from Amber. "Hello, Beth, I am calling to let you know I have sorted things out with my parents. We came to a compromise. I am not to let it be known I'm a lesbian until I have finished college. This will save mother's face with her fancy friends. Dad didn't seem to be worried, but he doesn't have much say. So, I'm calling to say thank you. I'm so grateful."

"That's great, Amber. You live your life as you want. Don't be persuaded by anyone else, otherwise it is not your own life. Good luck, my dear," I said to her.

"That went fine; a good result," I told myself.

I sat at my desk and daydreamed as it was a quiet afternoon. My mind kept taking me back to John. Would he be back tomorrow? I couldn't wait. Then I asked myself where he was going to stay. Would it be proper of me to ask him to stay with me if it was only for two nights? Was I taking the whole situation out of context? Was this just a one-night fling for John? I didn't want to think that was so, because it meant a lot to me, and I would be so disappointed if this was so. No, he didn't appear to me to be a taker, then neither had Phil. My choice of men was not a good recommendation. No, John was a gentleman and I'm sure he enjoyed our rendezvous as much as I did.

It was Friday, the day John was arriving back. I had no idea what time or of his intentions, but I guess that would sort itself out. I had two appointments in the morning and one straight after lunch. My staff had never let go of the fact that John and I had had sex. I tried to be discreet, but exuberance got the better of me. They both gave their stamp of approval and shared in my excitement of seeing him again.

With my appointments over, I was free for the rest of the afternoon, but I didn't want to leave the office in case John arrived. When four o'clock came and went, I started to think he wasn't coming back. Had I let my imagination run away with me? Perhaps it was just a one-night stand after all. I had a sinking feeling, as doubt was now taking over.

At five o'clock I said goodbye to the girls. They knew how down I was feeling so offered to stay on, but I told them to go home. Tears filled my eyes as I locked the office door. I climbed into my car, sat for a moment wondering if I should go the Angler's Arms, but decided to go home instead.

To my absolute delight there was John's car parked beside my driveway. I pushed the remote and the garage door opened for me to drive in. Next minute John was parked in my driveway. My heart was racing with excitement. He was back; he hadn't let me down!

"Hi Beth, it's lovely to be back. I thought I would call around before booking into the pub to see if you would come out for dinner with me. But first, what about a cuddle?"

"Don't rush," I told myself, but my legs got the better of me and I nearly bolted into his arms. We both held on, not wanting to break from our embrace. "Did you have a good time with your friend?" I asked. He explained they were army buddies and had both survived the bloody D-Day battle, although many of their friends had not, so it was a bittersweet reunion.

"Did you miss me?" I sheepishly asked.

"If you have to ask me that Beth, then you are not as worldly as I thought. Of course I missed you. You gave me the best night of my life. Don't you remember I told you that?'

I invited him in for a coffee or a wine. "No, I'll go and book in first so I get a bed for the night, then I will come back and pick you up."

"I would like you to stay with me. You don't need to go to a pub. That is, only if you want to of course."

"What do you mean if I want to? I would love to stay with you. I can't promise to behave myself though. If those terms suit, the answer is yes."

With this sorted we went inside. I made John coffee and he told me about his couple of days away. He asked how I got on with Amber's parents, so I explained everything. "Well, that was a good outcome, Beth, but that's your job to sort out other people's issues; you are the problem solver. I have an idea: let's go out for dinner then there is no cooking and no cleaning up afterwards.

I'll get my case out of the car and change into suitable attire."

Once we had both changed, we drove to a little Italian restaurant nearby. This was a chance to try new cuisine. We ordered different dishes so we could share. It felt like an intimate dinner as we both laughed and enjoyed ourselves. After a couple of wines, we drove home as John had had a big day of driving many miles, so bed was the story.

"You use the bathroom first, John, then jump into bed. I'll follow." When he had finished, I went to the bathroom. Then I heard him call, "Don't be long, Beth. I don't want to fall asleep and miss all the fun!" I laughed; he made the situation so much easier. As I showered, I let the hot water flow over my body, which was trembling with excitement. I got into my best nightie; it wasn't see-through or very sexy but how long was it going to stay on? Sexy didn't matter.

As I climbed into bed, John moved over to be near me and kissed my cheek. We snuggled into each other, then I felt his hands moving over my body, caressing me. I lay there and let it happen; it made me feel sexy, and my body came alive. Next thing I felt my nightie being pulled up, so I sat up and let John remove it. Now I was naked but this time there was no embarrassment, as it all felt natural. His hands slid down my thighs to my womanly parts, where they lingered. This was the trigger. I wanted him to feel what I was feeling so I reached for his manly organ, then it all happened. Between us we worked up a storm, there was a bolt of lightning, a roar of thunder and the jolt of an earthquake, then silence, the storm was over, and two loved-up adults lay contented in each other's arms.

When I woke the next morning, I was still naked, so I reached over to touch John, but he wasn't in bed. I sat up only to find him standing with a tray of toast and two cups of coffee, a bare chest and a towel wrapped around his waist. I asked him to put the tray on the dresser and come back to bed. He didn't take any persuading and as he came over, I whipped down the towel, leaving him standing there exposed. He laughed then jumped into bed to get his revenge.

By lunchtime the toast was soggy and the coffees were cold. We dressed and walked hand in hand to a nearby café. "I have to tell you, Beth, this has been the best part of my life since meeting you. I feel wanted and loved as well as happy and content. We have shared laughter as well as our bodies. I'm going to truly miss you."

"Do you have to go back so soon, John? Why can't you stay longer? My life will never be the same without you. I feel alive and excited, something I haven't felt for years," I pleaded.

"My flight is booked, and I have to get back to my work. The men will be counting on me as will the company. Also, my children will be anxious for me to come home. But if all these things were put together, they cannot give me what I have found here with you."

"What are we going to do, John, as we will be oceans apart?" I sobbed. With this we decided to walk home and talk things over.

For the rest of the afternoon and most of the night,

apart from a few disruptions that took place, we tried to work out a plan, but no final decisions could be made. This was the last night we would share my bed together, which brought tears from both parties. Now I was saying goodbye to my only bit of happiness I'd had in years. John put his case in the car then we clung to each other. "Goodbye my darling," John said as he let me go. I knew in my heart what I was feeling so I told him, "I love you, John."

Where was John?

My life had changed since John left. I felt empty and unhappy. My business was not fulfilling any more. Although I was at my office every day, sometimes it was a drag to get myself there. The spring in my step had gone, leaving me feeling lonely and sad. My happiness disappeared the day John left. There had been no contact between us since. All I knew about his life in New Zealand was that he worked for the Ford Motor Company, had three children and had had an unhappy marriage. Why hadn't I heard from him? Had he forgotten me already? Was this another happy period in my life that had gone horribly wrong? Had I fallen for the wrong guy once again? My choices were shit! I couldn't even live on memories any more. What curveball could life throw at me next?

I continued existing in a dazed world, of heartbreak and delusion. I carried on giving advice and helping people, but felt I was living a lie when my own house was not in order. I put on a brave front, although my staff saw through me. They tried to get me to have a holiday to forget John, but even a holiday couldn't cut it. How could I just forget the man who had been in most stages of my life? Even if it was in memory, he was still part of me. Happiness only seemed to stay with me for a short time, then it would disappear as quickly as it came.

I decided to take a week off and visit my children, James and Sarah, in London. I told them about John, and they were sympathetic towards me. Sarah took me shopping and tried to get me to buy new clothes, but I felt it was a waste of money as I had no one to go out with. I was told off for being stingy.

"Mother you have been there before and survived. You can do it again," Sarah told me. I knew she was trying to snap me out of my doldrums, but that wasn't going to be easy! Sarah had arranged for James to have lunch with us to see if he could cheer me up, as I think she thought I was a lost soul. James wanted to go an Italian lunch bar so off we went. As soon as I saw the menu it took me back to lunch out with John, and the tears started.

"Mother, what is wrong with you? You have never been beaten in your life, so please don't give in now. You are a strong person. Hold on to that strength. What happened to your meditation? That was meant to help you manage your life. Are you still practising it?"

Suddenly, I realised I hadn't been meditating for a couple of months. Perhaps that is what could get me through this rough patch I was facing.

"Thank you, James, yes when I was meditating, I could control my life, and nothing bothered me. I was calm and collected and could face adversity. From tomorrow I will begin back with it and see if I can throw off these blues."

"Good on you, Mother, that's what we want to hear, isn't it, Sarah?" From then on, I perked up. Yes, that was what was missing apart from John, but it looked like he was history.

I was back home and right into my meditation, and life was on a turn for the better. I told myself that if I didn't like myself how could I like anyone else? So, I had to build up my self-belief. Today was my appointment at the retreat. They were running a seven-day course on dealing with trauma. Thank goodness it was a few days, as it would take my thoughts away from John. I loved being a teacher. I had been to the retreat centre several times and got on really well with Joel; we understood each other.

There were ten people enrolled on the course. We planned that I would listen to their trauma-related cases, and talk them through it over the seven days, so there was no confusion. Then at the end of the course I would tell them about my traumatic life, and how I dealt with it. This course was like any other and involved healthy eating, meditation and massage classes. We would split into two groups, while one was dealing with trauma the other would be doing something else. Then we would swap.

As the people arrived, they were given their room key and their name badge which they had to wear all the time, while attending classes. Everybody was welcomed by the manager, Sophia, who assured everyone they would have a great experience and would take home positives from the course. Once checked in, it was then time to meet for a healthy lunch. Next it was off to their group sessions. In my first group I had three women and two men.

I introduced myself and asked if anyone had gone through some sort of trauma in their lives. All hands were raised. Most of my class were in their mid-fifties, but this was the age when marriages started to sour, and the men looked to younger women. I started by saying all traumas were treatable, but patients had to help themselves, as they were their own best healers. It was a matter of self-belief.

It surprised me to find four out of my group of five were going through marriage break-ups and that was the start of their trauma. The women's trauma started off with loneliness and lack of self-esteem. They felt themselves to be failures because they couldn't hold their marriages together. But, sadly, in most cases it was not their fault, as their partners had moved on to a younger woman. The men were the ones at fault, as they couldn't come to terms with the fact that as their wives age, so do they.

My second group consisted of four women and one man. The man had lost his wife and was traumatised by the thought of living on his own. He was living on memories, and he couldn't function in the real world; he just sat in a chair day after day. This was the wrong thing for him to be doing. He had to get out and talk with people, join a club or even walk to the pub and have a pint. But to shut off from life was the wrong thing to do, because he then had all the time in the world to pine for his wife. It's not what his wife would want.

There are so many traumatic things going on in people's lives, and the best cure is to turn inward and love yourself for whoever you are. You are unique, and there is only one of you. It is the healer of all setbacks, to start within, to love yourself first. At the end of each session, I told my story and this left people in horror and wonder how I was able to survive and be the person I was today. The short answer was meditation: to go to that peaceful place for twenty minutes a day, where there is just you … and you alone!

At the end of the course everyone left happy. Once they heard other people's traumas, they realised they were not on their own, that at some time in our lives, we all face something unexpected. Life goes on just the same, and we cannot save the world or everything in it; it is just not going to happen.

Now I was on my way home hoping for a miracle, or just some good news. What had happened to John? Had he given up on me? How could something so hot go so cold, so quickly? I had had my share of heartache, so surely happiness wasn't going to elude me forever. My choice of men hadn't done me any favours; they had let me down. John had been on my life's journey with me, and I thought a storybook ending was awaiting me … but was it?

One Friday morning the unexpected happened. My doorbell rang and when I opened the door there stood John! I was stunned, speechless, angry and ecstatic all at the same time. Then I let fly, "Why didn't you get in touch with me? My heart died the day we said goodbye. I have hardly been able to function … why John?"

"I'm sorry, Beth, I had to be sure that this was for all the right reasons. I'm not leaving England without you. Please come and live with me in New Zealand."

He did want me after all. I stood and looked at him; it was all too much so I burst into tears.

"Come here you daft thing, of course I want you. I love you. I have been working on this back home and once it was all settled, then I could make plans." With this I went to him, and we clung on to each other, neither wanting to let go.

John came inside and told me what had happened in New Zealand. He had resigned from the Ford Motor Company where he had worked for over forty years, and he was given a large bonus for his dedication to the company. He wanted to make a new life with me, so he had sold his home. He hated going back into it after leaving me, as all it brought back were sad memories of his loveless marriage. He told his daughters about me, and they were happy for him. Nothing was said to his son Michael as he would not understand fully about his father's situation. It would be unsettling for him.

"All you have to do is agree to come and live with me in New Zealand. What do you say, Beth?" I was surprised and ecstatic and took no time in answering him. "John, I accept to be your live-in lover, to love and cherish you forever. In simple English that means … yes!"

I didn't have to worry about James and Sarah, as they

would probably be happy that someone was taking me off their hands, after my last visit. But I would have to take the photos of my darling Alice with me, as I still felt I had to protect her. Then I suddenly realised that if I went to New Zealand, I couldn't visit her grave and talk to her. Would this mean I was going to forget her, and who would look after her? My heart felt torn.

I would have to decide about the future of my business. I was the person that attended to the clients and helped solve their problems, so it wouldn't be a business if I wasn't there. I decided to ask my staff if they wanted to take it over, but like me, they knew I was the business, so their answer was no. I decided I would close up shop after I had seen to all my bookings, so we stopped taking any more appointments. It would be sad, but in the last month I had learnt if one is not happy, a business is worth nothing. I would put the office and land up for sale, as it was prime real estate.

The next few weeks were like a whirlwind, and at night my bed became a love nest, and the days flew by. I had taken my last appointment so the 'For Sale' sign went up on the property. Within a week it had been snapped up by a developer who wanted to take the building down and put a multi-storey building on the site. I was sad to say goodbye to my two staff members, so we went out for dinner, and I gave them both a month's wages plus their holiday pay.

In between times we were trying to get a visa and the proper permits for me to live in New Zealand. It was going to make it easier if we were a married couple, so we took the plunge and had a quiet ceremony. Now I had a new title, I was Mrs Beth Wentworth. I rang the kids to let them know and they were happy for us. The spring had come back in my step, my brain had settled down and I was on top of the world. The only thought that crossed my mind was John was ten years older than me, which was a big gap, but what the hell…we had to make hay while the sun still shone, and happiness was what reigned supreme. My happiness had been short and sharp up until now, so I was going to make the most of what I could get.

But there was still the thought of Alice being on her own. I called Sarah and James and asked them if they would visit Alice's grave and take her flowers. Even if it was just every month.

"Mother, you go and live the rest of your life being happy. James and I will take flowers to Alice's grave. You have her photo so you can still talk to her. I wish we could have met John, then we wouldn't have to worry. Would you both come and see us before you leave, please?"

I talked over with John about meeting James and Sarah, and he agreed. It would easier for them to accept their mother going to live in another country if they met him. He could understand that they would be worried. It was planned that John and I would catch the train to London, as neither of us were keen to drive, and James would pick us up at London Charing Cross as he lived near Trafalgar Square, so that was the closest station.

We alighted from the train and stood on the platform not knowing in which direction to go. John asked where the main exit to the station was, so a friendly man told us to follow him, as that was where he was heading. There to meet us was James and Sarah. Sarah ran to me and hugged me, then introductions were in order. James had booked us into a hotel nearby, as his flat only had one bedroom.

The four of us had dinner at the hotel so we could get to know each other. James asked John a lot of questions and said he hoped that he would look after his mother as she had coped with a lot of suffering.

"The moment I saw Beth I was attracted to her. All our lives we have thought about each other, and as it turned out, neither of us has been truly happy. I promise to love and care for your mother. She has brought so much joy to my heart, I'm grateful to have found her, as together we can have a happy life. I hope we have your and Sarah's blessings; it would be a magical end for us both." There were glasses raised and cheers all round. "To John and Beth, we wish you a happy life together," echoed James and Sarah.

Just before I left England, as I was his ex-wife I received the news that Phil had passed away. A letter was delivered by the courts as he had put me as next of kin. There were some of his belongings waiting to be picked up at the prison, and an amount of money in a bank account. He had made some toys in his woodwork class, and I was asked what I wanted done with them. I was numb, I didn't want anything of his but thought perhaps I had better call the kids. Their answer was the same as mine. Then I had a thought: perhaps Julie might be interested so I put a call through to her. I hadn't been in touch since the retreat, but I still had her phone number.

"Hi Julie, how are you and Alice? I have just been informed that Phil has passed away and there are some wooden toys he has made, and a bank account with money in it. Are you interested in any of his gear?"

"I do have grandchildren that might be interested in the toys. How much is in the bank account?" she asked. I told her I didn't know, but if she was interested in the toys, I could arrange for it to be picked up and delivered to her. "I may as well get something out of him. Are you sure that's okay with you?" she wanted to know. I assured her it was fine with me. Now all I had to do was make arrangements with the prison to have everything delivered to her.

My new homeland

It was a long flight to New Zealand, so I found it very draining. Sitting for nineteen hours was not in my nature. But with John by my side, holding my hand, I felt safe and content. He brought a calmness to me. I was going to live the rest of my life enjoying each day and being thankful for having been given another chance at happiness. A new life lay ahead!

After arriving in Wellington, John hailed a taxi to take us to a hotel he had booked for us. His daughters were coming the next night to have dinner with us and to meet me. I hope they approved of me. The next day I slept for most of it, as jetlag had caught up with me.

With John's girls dining with us, it would be strange to meet my namesake, Beth. I was also quite nervous wondering how they felt about their father finding someone else, after their mother had passed away. But soon I would know!

John and I made our way down to the house bar to meet them. John called to them. "Hi Beth, hi Shelley, come and meet my Beth." The girls gave me a hug. "Welcome to New Zealand, we hope you and Dad will be very happy." John had let them know we had got married, to help simplify my visa entry. The greeting came as a pleasant surprise to me, as I expected some resistance. "Thank you, girls, for making me feel so welcome."

We were shown to our table, so we ordered a drink each, and then chose our meal. The girls knew our background, as John had told them the story of the war years. The eldest, Beth, asked me, "Did you ever imagine your lives would connect again?" I told her John had always been in my life, as I had often wondered if he was happy, especially in my down moments. But no, I never imagined this would happen. It was as if fate had intervened. Then Shelley asked, "Did you know it was Dad when you first met him?"

"No, I had no idea. I stood and looked at him and when he said who he was, I was in shock. You must remember I was only young when I last saw John. He would have been about fifteen when he came to live with us. He invited me to his lodgings for dinner and we caught up on each other's lives."

"That's a lovely story," said Shelley. We chatted all through our meal. The girls were friendly towards me so I couldn't have wished for a better outcome.

"What have you guys got planned?" asked Beth. John replied, "I am taking Beth on a tour of the South Island, and we will look for a quiet place to settle and perhaps get a little business that we can work in together. By that time Beth's container will have landed at the port, then we can think about setting up house somewhere. Beth and I haven't discussed anything as yet, but do these arrangements sound okay to you, my dear?"

"I am in your hands, John, as I know nothing about my new country, but it all sounds exciting to me." As the night came to an end, the girls gave us both a hug and wished us all the best. We apparently were leaving the next morning. We went back to our suite, undressed and snuggled up in bed. Nothing energetic would be on the cards tonight. Sleep would reign.

Today was the beginning of my travels in my new country. A friend of John's dropped his car off at the hotel, as we had to be up and away and be somewhere by 11.30am. This was my first glimpse of Wellington, although it was to be short, as John wouldn't tell me where we were going. I was just an observer. I took in all my surroundings, as we seemed to be heading downtown towards what looked like the wharf. There were railway lines everywhere, then I saw cars and trucks lined up waiting to go somewhere.

"What are we waiting here for?" I asked.

"See that ferry. We are going to drive onto it, and it will take us across Cook Strait to the South Island." As the line of vehicles started to move, and we got closer to where we were to drive onto the ferry, I was happy John was driving. There were men waving their hands while some were yelling. You almost had to be a mind reader to understand all their signals.

Once the car was secure in its place, we made our way up a couple of decks and found a seat by a window. John told me we were lucky it was a pleasant day, as Cook Strait was renowned for its rough crossings. He told me about the tragedy of a ferry that had capsized in a storm with many lives lost. The sea was quite calm, although the odd large wave broke across the bow sending spray over the deck. I was happy I was inside the cabin.

As we left the open sea and entered the Marlborough Sounds, we seemed to be very close to land at times, so we ventured out on to the open deck and took in the beauty surrounding us. With John's arms around me I felt safe and closed my eyes and breathed in the fresh smell of sea air. As we docked, we were asked to make our way to our vehicles. Once again, I was happy that I was the passenger, as those arm-waving men were yelling orders for people to follow, to get their cars off the ferry.

John told me we had arrived in Picton, and we were going to drive to a town called Blenheim, where we were booked into a hotel for the night. On the way, I was surprised to see vineyards as I thought the wine was grown in the North Island, but John corrected me on that, as some of the largest vineyards were in Marlborough. We arrived at our hotel and booked in, then went to the inhouse restaurant. John wanted me to try a local wine with my meal, so asked the bartender to choose a good local one. I had to admit it was very nice and it went well with my steak.

After we had eaten, we went up to our room and I chose to use the bathroom first. As I was showering, John came in and decided to share the shower with me. We soaped each other and then the caressing started. It wasn't long before we turned off the water and hurriedly tried to dry each other, so we could make it to the bed while we were both eager to make love. This was our first sex session in the South Island. I loved it when John took me, as I felt a complete woman. For so long these feelings had lain dormant and now they had been reawakened. It made me sad to think all those years I had wasted, but then again, I didn't have anyone to make love with!

The next day we were driving to Kaikoura which I thought was a funny name until John explained it was Māori. As we left Blenheim, we saw many vineyards. I was amazed how much of the land was planted out and it wasn't all flat land; the vines were growing on the side of hills and in valleys. I had only seen small holdings of vines in England. These vineyards stretched for miles upon miles. I was intrigued.

As we drove on, we followed the coastline until we reached Kaikoura. John drove round the sea front to see if we could catch a whale boat that was taking visitors whale spotting. But alas they had finished for the day as there had been no sightings. Once settled into our motel we relaxed for an hour then John wanted to find a café that had crayfish on the menu. I had never eaten crayfish as it was like gold in England. I agreed to try a piece if John ordered it, but no ... he wasn't sharing his crayfish with me; I had to have my own meal. So, to keep him happy I ordered the same as his. I hoped I liked it otherwise John would have to consume a double dose of crayfish, not that he would have protested. I was most surprised when the meal came out how inviting it looked, and I have to say it was delicious. I could see why John would not want to share his dinner with me.

For the first time, I noticed a guitar on the back seat of John's car. "Why is the guitar travelling with us?" I asked him.

"I play the guitar and sing. What is your singing voice like?"

I told him it was okay, but because my life was quite dismal at times I had forgotten how to sing. I knew you had to feel happy to put out a good song. "Okay, tonight we will have a practice and see how we sound together," he replied. I laughed as I thought he was being silly. But when we got back to the motel out came the guitar, and it came inside with us. We settled in and he started strumming and singing and I was very impressed. I hadn't known he could sing, but then again it was never discussed, and we were a new couple, so there were still plenty of things to find out about each other. John invited me to join him in his singing, so I gave it a go and we sounded okay. John was great, but I was a bit rusty.

"A few practices and we will be great together. Perhaps one day we could entertain the elderly for sing-alongs. They like all the old songs, the ones from yesteryear, the ones we remember," he said with a grin.

"You will remember ones further back than I remember," I joked.

After travelling around the South Island and seeing so many beautiful places, I was sold on New Zealand. The tourist towns were lovely to visit, but I could not live in them, as the congestion of traffic, especially in Queenstown, was too much. Also, I couldn't believe the wineries this far south, as once again there were acres upon acres of them. "Gosh, the people of New Zealand must consume a lot of wine. What do they do with it all?" I asked. I then learnt a lot of it was exported all over the world, and that it was very popular. New Zealand was renowned for its good wines. Then I remembered seeing a lot of it on the shelves in the supermarkets in England, but I hadn't taken a lot of notice, not thinking for one moment I would be living here one day.

John was fascinated with the cycleways that took people off the beaten track, into the back of beyond. Everywhere we came in contact with them they were busy with cyclists, and the little towns' eating places were full of enthusiastic people having a wonderful time. We stayed at a town called Clyde which was where one end of the Rail Trail began before it went through the Maniototo region of Central Otago and finished at the town of Middlemarch. This was another end of the Rail Trail, so we were able to find all the information that interested John.

The next day we drove on to Omakau and got little glimpses of the Rail Trail along the way, where it came in sight of the road. There were always people on it. We then stopped at Oturehua, where the little pub was buzzing, as the cyclists were taking a break to have lunch. Our next stop was Ranfurly, but we didn't see much of the Rail Trail as it went through farms away from the main highway.

John was intrigued by the number of people that had chosen to use this cycle trail. There were people of all ages, children, adults, even elderly people being pulled along in buggies by cyclists, probably family members, but they all had something in common and that was a smile on their face. When we caught up with groups of cyclists, they all had the same story, that it was the best thing they had done, as they were seeing country that was not seen from the highway. There were little accommodation places all along the trail where people could stop off and spend the night to break the journey.

We stopped at Ranfurly for the night and spoke with cyclists who were also having a break, as they were pretty sore, having been on the bike all day. The next day we were heading to Middlemarch. We stopped at a little place called Hyde, and it was swamped with bicycles as riders were taking a well-earned break to eat. This was the last stop of any consequence before Middlemarch. When we arrived at Middlemarch there was very little there. It was a small settlement in the middle of nowhere! There were a couple of cafés and not much else. We found a camping ground called Blind Billys, so booked in for a night or two, but we weren't sure how long we would be here. It was a farming community, and it was an alternate route from Central Otago to Dunedin. I wondered what the womenfolk did, but most would be farmers' wives I guessed. The lady from the camp told us there were a few retired people residing in the area, and it was a friendly community.

John was taken by the area, as it was peaceful, yet there

was always something happening as the cyclists congregated in the cafés at the end of their ride. The Taieri train would bring people from Dunedin either with their bikes or they would hire bikes in Middlemarch, to begin their Rail Trail journey ending at Clyde. The cyclists that started at Clyde would catch the train back to Dunedin. It was a two-way trip. John asked me to get into the car so we could drive around and explore, to see if I felt I could settle here, as he had good vibes about the area.

As we drove down the road, we came across a house with a 'For Sale' sign so John stopped outside. "I'll just go and enquire and see what the story is, and what price is on the property," he told me. I sat in the car thinking to myself: "Do I think I could live here?" But then I had to remind myself that as long as we were together that was all that mattered. Next thing there was a knock on the window and John wanted me to come and have a look inside the house. He explained that the people were shifting out next week, so all their belongings were packed, but we could have a look through. It was a quaint little place and out the back was a large area with a hen house and some chickens which went with the property. John told the people we would think about it over the next couple of days, then we would give them an answer.

That night we talked about the property; John was really keen. "Is there enough to keep us busy here? What would we do?" I asked. Obviously, John had been wondering that too.

"We will contact the retirement villages in Dunedin

and see if they would like us to entertain. Also, I had the bright idea of us building a private croquet pitch, as there isn't one here. Farming communities like sporting venues as it brings them together. We will buy a little bulldozer and I will do the earthmoving, then we can potter with it ourselves. What do you think?"

I wasn't sure. Then I thought, if that was what John wanted to do, I would back him all the way, because as long as we were together, did it really matter where we lived? We went back to the people who were selling their house and told them we would buy it. My container had arrived in Wellington so now we had to get it shipped to Dunedin, then it would have to be transported to Middlemarch.

Now we were settled in our little house with the chooks. They kept us in eggs, and we put in a vegetable garden. John had bought a piece of land for us to start our venture. He managed to buy a little bulldozer so was on it each day levelling out the land. We had been asked to entertain at several of the retirement villages in Dunedin, so we needed to practise our singing, which we did at night. We had lots of laughs, and at times when John felt amorous, he would serenade me to the bedroom. We were still very much in love.

Today was our first gig, so we had to drive to Dunedin and be at the home by two o'clock. We left early and visited a grocery shop to stock up until we next came to the city. We sang all the old songs the elderly remembered. Some went to sleep while others sang along with us. In all, it was a good day, and we were invited back in two weeks to entertain.

Day after day we spent many hours setting up our croquet pitch. John had purchased another house that we shifted to the pitch to use as a clubhouse. In between times we were driving to Dunedin to fulfil our rest home appointments, which we enjoyed as we met new people. What John didn't realise was we were also growing older. He was almost the same age as those in the rest homes, the ones we were entertaining.

Our lives were very busy; why did I ever think we would have nothing to do to occupy our minds, when we came to this little out-of-the-way place? We enjoyed meeting the locals and made good friends. Running the croquet pitch was fun. It was a private club, but we invited teams from outlying districts to come and play. This life suited us as we were kept busy maintaining the pitch and mixing with people.

Sadly, the age difference between John and me was starting to show. The grounds work was becoming too much for him. This was the time when we had to reassess our lives and make plans for our future. Because we loved entertaining at the rest homes, we saw how happy the people were who lived in them, and we decided this was the life for us.

One year on, we were in our new home in a retirement village, and it didn't take long to make friends, as we knew a lot of the residents. We still had a yearning to travel but as driving was out for John, we joined the Sunshine Travel Club, a company that took one-day trips as well as three to four-day tours. This suited us fine; we could still stay in touch with the outside world.

One trip stays in my mind. A woman on the bus in the seat opposite was talking to us and John happened to mention he met me as a five year old. This intrigued her, so she asked John to explain. He told her it had all begun during the Second World War in England when the Germans were Blitzing the East End of London. It so happened this person on the bus was an author who then asked if she could write a book on our lives. She found what we had told her very interesting, and it had the core of a good story … we only told her our beginning and the ending; the in-between is her story.

Also by Margaret Nyhon

Fiction

Isobella (Book 1 in the *Isobella* series)

Isobella: Self Redemption (Book 2 in the *Isobella* series)

Papa's Girl Emmeline

Betrayal by an Irish Rose

Revenge for an English Lord (sequel to *Betrayal by an Irish Rose*)

For Girls' Eyes Only

Daughters Lost to the Underworld

Pimchan and Amira

Coronavirus: A Novel

The Whistle-blower's Severed Link (sequel to *Coronavirus: A Novel*)

Fortune Smiles as Love Divides

The Stolen Girl (sequel to *Fortune Smiles as Love Divides*)

Non-fiction

de Marisco

Freedom Knows No Boundaries

A Wake-up Call

A Shattered Dream Across the Tasman

Memories and Moving On

About the Author

Margaret Nyhon lives in Mosgiel, New Zealand, where she writes, paints and practises the crafts of printing and bookbinding.

She has worked extensively in hospitality management in New Zealand and resort management in Australia. The urge to trace her family history led her to the writing of her first non-fiction work, *de Marisco*. She has since written several fiction and non-fiction books. Margaret is married and has three adult children and two grandsons.

Contact Margaret: margaretf@hotmail.co.nz

www.ingramcontent.com/pod-product-compliance
Lightning Source LLC
Chambersburg PA
CBHW020942310726
48980CB00001B/14